LULU DARK

DARK

AND THE
SUMMER OF
THE FOX

Also by Bennett Madison

Lulu Dark Can See Through Walls

LULU DARK
AND THE SUMMER OF THE FOX

A MYSTERY BY

BENNETT MADISON

SLEUTH
RAZORBILL

Lulu Dark and the Summer of the Fox

RAZORBILL

Published by the Penguin Group
Penguin Young Readers Group
345 Hudson Street, New York, New York 10014, U.S.A.
Penguin Group (USA) Inc., 375 Hudson Street, New York, New York 10014, U.S.A.
Penguin Group (Canada), 90 Eglinton Avenue East, Suite 700, Toronto,
Ontario, Canada M4P 2Y3 (a division of Pearson Penguin Canada Inc.)
Penguin Books Ltd, 80 Strand, London WC2R 0RL, England
Penguin Ireland, 25 St Stephen's Green, Dublin 2, Ireland
(a division of Penguin Books Ltd)
Penguin Group (Australia), 250 Camberwell Road, Camberwell,
Victoria 3124, Australia (a division of Pearson Australia Group Pty Ltd)
Penguin Books India Pvt Ltd, 11 Community Centre, Panchsheel Park, New Delhi - 110 017, India
Penguin Group (NZ), Cnr Airborne and Rosedale Roads, Albany, Auckland 1310,
New Zealand (a division of Pearson New Zealand Ltd)
Penguin Books (South Africa) (Pty) Ltd, 24 Sturdee Avenue, Rosebank,
Johannesburg 2196, South Africa

Penguin Books Ltd, Registered Offices: 80 Strand, London WC2R 0RL, England

10 9 8 7 6 5 4 3 2 1

Interior design by Christopher Grassi

THE LIBRARY OF CONGRESS HAS CATALOGED THE HARDCOVER EDITION AS FOLLOWS:
Madison, Bennett.
 Lulu Dark and the summer of the Fox : a mystery / by Bennett Madison.
   p. cm.
 Summary: When a mysterious person called the Fox begins to threaten young starlets, Lulu Dark
investigates, even though she suspects that her own mother—an aging actress—might be behind it all.
 ISBN 1-59514-086-7
 [1. Actors and actresses—Fiction. 2. Mothers and daughters—Fiction. 3. Interpersonal
relations—Fiction. 4. Mystery and detective stories. 5. Humorous stories.] I. Title.
 PZ7.M26Ltd 2006
 [Fic]—dc22
                                                                2006004960

Razorbill Splashproof paperback ISBN 978-1-59514-154-5

Manufactured in China

*For my mother, who should be happy
to find that she is not in this book*

ONE

IT WAS ABOUT TO STORM, AND Daisy and I were dressed like we were on our way to a croquet match. The first real thunderstorm of the summer and we were going to be caught in it—without umbrellas, raincoats, or even long sleeves. We were totally defenseless. We couldn't have cared less.

It was a quarter after noon on a previously gorgeous day, and my best friend and I were headed out for lunch when the sun just, like, turned black. Daisy was wearing a pastel pink caftan, baby blue flip-flops, and enormous plastic Jackie O sunglasses from the drugstore. I was decked out in black stretch pants, a white cotton wraparound tunic, and my favorite hot pink cowboy boots.

On second thought, I suppose we *didn't* look like we were headed to a croquet match, but it wasn't exactly hurricane gear either. There on the corner of Washington and Church, three blocks from where she lived, Daisy and I turned our attention to the ominous, all-encompassing cloud that was standing in for the sky. Halo City was suddenly hushed. Up and down the most bustling stretch of Washington Avenue everyone was doing the same thing—looking up.

"Well," Daisy said.

"Well," I said.

There was a clap of thunder and a drop of rain, then two at once.

"There goes my hairdo," Daisy said.

On that particular day my best friend had fixed her hair into an elaborate tiara of curls. She did indeed look insane. Insane, yet weirdly awesome. And kind of beautiful, too. That has always been part of Daisy's charm.

I wish I could get away with wearing a caftan in public. Do you know how comfortable those things are?

Two more drops of rain and then it all started to come down, I mean really come down, and all we could do was laugh and keep strolling as it soaked us. We didn't even bother picking up our pace. Why should we? That day, to me, a rainstorm meant only one thing.

"It's finally summer!" I cheered. I pulled the rubber band out of my ponytail and shook out my wet hair as Daisy hopped across a newly formed puddle on the corner into the street. She laughed and pointed at me. I looked down. My white tunic was becoming plastered to my torso and quickly turning transparent. Oh well.

"I don't care," I said. "A thunderstorm out of nowhere is the perfect way to start our vacation. School is over and we can frolic in the rain if we want to. A few losers on Washington Avenue seeing my bra is the last thing I'm worried about. I'm feeling too celebratory to care."

"You deserve it, Lulu, after all you've been through," Daisy said. "It's time for a well-earned vacation."

My junior year at Orchard Academy had finished off with, shall we say, a bang. A big bang. I'm not going to go into too much detail, but the bottom line is that having your purse stolen is traumatic. Having your purse stolen by a criminally psychotic wanna-be scenester who also has taken your identity, your reputation, and your rock-star would-be boyfriend is *not* traumatic. It's . . . I don't know, it's just so much worse than that. I tried to find a word for it in my thesaurus, but there isn't one. At least, not one that doesn't belittle the plight of POWs and victims of famine. I guess we can just call it *beyond suck.*

Now that school was out and vacation had arrived, I felt incredibly relieved. I had plans, big plans—and by big I mean unspeakably small. I would *not* be slinking through dark alleys, staking out apartment buildings, or partaking in any other crime-solving activities.

Instead I'd be watching daytime television, talking on the telephone, and lying on the fire escape in my bikini. Frolicking in the rain would do in a pinch.

"This is going to be the least exciting summer ever," I declared happily.

"We should be so lucky," Daisy said. And a huge bolt of lightning shot through the sky.

"Golf clap," I said. Together Daisy and I broke out into subdued, polite applause. My days of girl detection were so over.

Or so I hoped.

But then out of nowhere, in the downpour, Daisy's jaw dropped.

She let out a loud gasp. Or maybe it was a screech or a cross between the two. Either way, she grabbed my hand and jerked me into an alley without so much as a "Hey, let's take a look in this dark, scary alley!"

The rain came down harder. I could barely see five feet ahead of me. My boots were filling with swampy water, and Daisy was saying, "Lulu, don't panic!"

"Why would I panic?" I asked. "It's just a little rain. And what are you shoving me around for?"

"We're being followed!" Daisy yelped. "There's a goon hot on our trail!"

"Oh, please." I sighed. "This is not *Veronica Mars*. In real life, mysteries happen once in a lifetime, not once a week. No one is following us." I tried to untangle myself from her grip, but she just pulled tighter.

"Lulu, this is serious," she hissed. "Someone is definitely following us. I bet Hattie Marshall escaped from the loony bin and is coming to get us!"

The mention of my purse snatcher and erstwhile alter ego's name sent a shiver down my spine.

"No. It couldn't be!" I wheezed.

"It could!" Daisy said, nodding furiously. "It definitely could!"

I cast my gaze around the alley for a way out—but we were hiding in a dead end. A rainy, disgusting, smelly dead end.

An explosion of thunder rattled the fire escapes above us. I nearly jumped out of my skin. We had to get out of there before I was face-to-face with the girl who, barely more than a month before, had tried to push me onto live subway tracks. Among other things.

"Quick, under there," I said, pointing to a dirty blue tarp scrunched into a corner of the alleyway. We raced to it and scurried under it, making ourselves as small as possible so as to be inconspicuous.

Huddled together in the pouring rain in a dark alley under a tarp, Daisy and I just looked at each other. Her face, what I could see of it, was cast in the blue of the plastic sheet, and if the situation hadn't been so dire, I would certainly have laughed at the fact that she was still wearing her cheapo sunglasses. The sound of raindrops on top of us sounded like pennies against a glass window.

"At least it's dry under here," Daisy whispered.

"Yeah, except for my butt!" I replied.

Sitting on wet pavement is not exactly comfortable. When you're wearing stretch pants and a white tunic, it's also a poor fashion decision—not that *that* was on my mind.

No, at that particular moment I was more concerned with the fact that my arch-nemesis was after me and could potentially be planning to kill me.

"How much did you see of the person who was following us?" I asked, trying to assess the situation.

"I don't know," Daisy whispered. "Her face was hidden behind a black umbrella. Plus it's hard to see in this kind of weather."

"Especially in sunglasses," I pointed out.

"That too," Daisy admitted. "But it definitely looked like a woman. And Hattie *is* a woman! I'm sure it was her."

Sometimes with Daisy you really have to spell things out.

"Um—what exactly gave you the impression that this supposed woman was following us at all?" I asked.

"I could just tell!"

I frowned. This was starting to feel like one of Daisy's "hunches." Otherwise known as her imagination.

"Come on, Daisy. You mean you just figured that—" I began to lift the blue tarp to make my escape.

That's when I heard them—footsteps. Chunky, sensible heels clomping on the asphalt, getting closer. Daisy clutched me and yelped. Maybe she had been on to something after all. I dug my fingernails into her bicep.

Cloppety cloppety cloppety CLOMP CLOMP CLOMP.

The sound grew louder. The mystery stalker drew closer. The stomping came to an abrupt halt. Our pursuer was right in front of us.

Our tarp rustled and was whisked away.

Daisy and I screamed at the top of our lungs.

Standing right over us, tarp in one hand, black umbrella in the other, was one of the most terrifying people I've ever met in my whole entire life.

Daisy's mother, Svenska.

TWO

DAISY TOOK IN HER MOTHER'S face, turned to me, and screamed even louder.

The elder Turner just stood there, glaring, and I couldn't help but shudder. A mean look from that woman is something to behold. Half the time I expect lasers to shoot out of her eyes.

"On the grave of my dead father," Svenska fumed, her Dutch accent stronger than usual, "what kind of a daughter have I raised? Get up off the ground, you two; people will think you're homeless."

She paused for a moment and narrowed her eyes. "Homeless *or worse*," she amended.

Daisy didn't stand. She tried to grab the tarp from her mother's clutch, but Svenska wasn't having it. "Why were you following us, *Mother*?" Daisy asked, giving her best turn at petulance.

It was unconvincing. Daisy isn't good at playing the attitude card. It just isn't in her nature.

Svenska's eyes seemed to do a complete 360 in their sockets. "Following you? *Following you?* That's a good one." She snorted.

Daisy and I sat there, staring. My carefree attitude toward the rain was waning. Wetness, as a concept, was starting to get old. Rain was pouring down my face, I couldn't see, and I could taste my own eyeliner.

It tasted bad.

"You mean you *weren't* following us?" Daisy asked her mother pointedly.

"For your information, young lady, I wanted to give you an umbrella." Ignoring the torrential downpour, Svenska closed her umbrella, shook it out, and tossed it at Daisy. "I mean, for goodness sake. You two look like drowned rats."

Daisy sat silent on the pavement, sullenly examining the umbrella.

"Drowned rats, that's what you look like!" Svenska ranted. "Both of you were just asking for trouble—leaving the house without an umbrella or even a simple, solitary raincoat between you on a summer afternoon? It's as if you wanted it! I ask you, who wants to be a drowned rat? Who wants to be a drowned rat but a couple of dumb bunnies?"

And on Svenska's last syllable, the rain ended. Just like that. The sun came out, and it was as though it had never stormed in the first place.

The three of us looked up at the sky.

"Well," Daisy said.

"Well," I said.

Svenska looked deflated. "That's what you are," she muttered, the wind out of her sails. "Just a couple of dumb bunnies."

"You can have this back," Daisy said. She slicked her drenched bangs behind her ear and offered the umbrella up to her mother with a smirk.

"Keep it!" Svenska screamed—and I'm not exaggerating when I

say that she screamed. The whole city probably heard it. Two miles away my father was probably shaking his head ruefully.

Toby Dark thinks Svenska is the most hilarious thing ever to happen to the world. Personally, I think he could try to be a little sympathetic to poor Daisy.

Svenska spun on her heel and clomped back out of the alleyway.

I took a deep breath, the first I'd dared take since the crazy Dutchwoman had discovered us.

"I'm wet and miserable," Daisy said when her mother was out of sight. She smacked the umbrella against a trash can.

"Me too," I said.

We sighed and slumped against whatever random building we were sitting under. And then we just started to laugh. We had to. Summer was off to a good start.

Two hours later Daisy and I were sitting in the garden at Little Edie's drinking our after-lunch coffee. The storm had passed as quickly as it started. It was gorgeous and green and sunny, and the birds were chirping in the trees above us like cute animal sidekicks in a Disney cartoon.

The bright June sun had made quick work of drying our clothes, and the only way you could have known there had been a near typhoon was the fact that Daisy's thick blond hair was still damp and wild looking.

Together we were working a crossword puzzle.

"'Rich in clay'?" Daisy quizzed me, perusing the clues.

"Loamy," I said, with no hesitation.

Daisy's brows knit together. "What in the world is a *loamy*?"

"I don't really know." I shrugged. "But they always use that one."

"Hmmm." Daisy filled in the letters without further question. "How about 'Garbo and Van Susteren'? Blank, *e*, blank, blank, *a*, blank."

"Gretas," I said.

"Wow. You're good," Daisy said. She looked the puzzle over. "Okay, you'll never get this one. 'Overbearing, irrational witch.': *S*, *v*, blank, blank, blank, *k*, blank." She lowered her sunglasses to the tip of her nose and gave me a wry look.

I giggled. "That's a little harsh, don't you think?"

But Daisy wasn't contrite. "No. The answer is my evil mother *Svenska* and I'm sick of it. That woman is crazy. And she was *not* trying to give me an umbrella. She was spying on us. She wanted to see where we were going."

"We told her where we were going," I pointed out.

"You think she believed us? She's the most paranoid person I ever met. She was probably afraid we were going to Dagger Pier to score ketamine or something. Whenever she thinks I'm acting weird, she asks me if I'm 'in a k-hole.' I think she read about it in *Newsweek* or saw it on *Dateline* or something. I gave her this book called *101 Conspiracy Theories* for her birthday as a joke, and she's still quoting it three months later."

Daisy put on her Svenska accent. "'Lieveling, did you know that the moon landing was nothing but a hoax?'"

"Next year you should give her a tinfoil beanie," I suggested.

"Good idea." Daisy nodded. "Maybe it would help her sort out her thoughts."

I raised my eyebrows. "Listen, Daisy. Count your blessings. At least your mother cares where you're going. Half the time I think my mother couldn't pick me out in a police lineup. I ask you: Which is worse?"

Daisy poured more sugar in her coffee and twisted her mouth to one side of her face.

I changed the subject. I hate talking about my mother.

"Charlie should be here soon," I said gloomily, checking my watch.

"Yay!" Daisy cheered.

"Not 'yay,'" I countered. "'Ugh' is more like it. Why didn't anyone tell me that having a boyfriend was going to be such a big responsibility? If I'd wanted to take care of another living creature, I would have gotten myself knocked up. At least with a baby you get to pick the name and dress it in funny outfits."

"Charlie would let you dress him in funny outfits." Daisy shrugged.

I sighed. "That's exactly the problem."

I was a little fuzzy on how I'd wound up with a boyfriend at all. To me, the idea of a boyfriend had always seemed like a pleasant abstraction, like having a pony or a Rolls-Royce or a cereal bowl made from solid gold.

Frankly, though, I'd never been desperate for any of those things. And even if I'd wanted a boyfriend, Charlie Reed would have been the last person to cross my mind.

Yet somehow here we were: official Boyfriend and Girlfriend.

Charlie and I had been friends, with a lowercase *f,* for practically my entire life, but somewhere in the last year things had gotten really mixed up. As in romantically.

It was weird. We'd grown up together, gone to school together, and even taken baths together when we were little. Now, after all these years, I was suddenly expected to allow this person to put his tongue in my mouth.

It was a little disconcerting, but I'd be lying if I said it was completely unpleasant.

The thing is, I *did* like Charlie. I mean, I'd always liked him as a friend, but to my surprise and consternation, I was starting to like him the other way too. *Carnally*, as my insane mother would say— but let's face it: using disgusting terms like that is exactly what makes her insane.

Anyway, attraction wasn't the problem. Charlie is hot. He just is. He's tall and wiry and sleepy-eyed, with floppy hair and a wry, romantic smirk. And he's sweet and smart and funny and oh yeah, one more thing—so rich that he could buy both of the Olsen twins and keep them in a glass case in his living room if he wanted to.

So really, aside from our personal history together, he should have been the perfect boyfriend. There was just one little problem.

"He will not leave me alone," I told Daisy. "I mean, he really *will not leave me alone*! I have to turn off my phone just to get a little peace and quiet."

I fished my celly from my beloved, tacky, recently recovered purse and powered it on. "Look!" I said, sliding it across the table.

Daisy flipped it open and bit her lip nervously. "Whoa. Five missed calls in two hours?"

"That's not even the start of it," I said. "He's completely lost his personality since we first kissed! He says, 'Let's go to the movies,' and I'm like, 'Okay! What movie?' and he's like, 'What movie do *you* want to see?' And I'm like, 'I don't know, what were you thinking of?' and he's like, 'Whatever would make me happy, Lulu!' And I'm like, 'For the love of God, have an opinion or I'm going to kill myself!'"

Daisy said nothing. She put on her poker face.

"Aaaghhh!" I exclaimed when I didn't get a reaction out of her. "I'm going completely insane!"

"Are you done having a total spaz?" she asked with a smirk. "Do you want me to spritz you down with some water?"

"Aaaghhh!" I shouted again, dropping my teaspoon with a clatter and throwing my hands into the air. The girl at the table next to us turned her head and glared. I looked straight at her and crossed my eyes until she looked away.

"I don't know what to say," Daisy told me. Her coffee was long gone, but she was still sipping at it like something was there. "Charlie is my friend too. I mean, I just don't think I can be impartial here."

"Couldn't you at least *try*?" I begged. "Who am I supposed to talk to about this otherwise? We all know that my mother is no use, even if I could get hold of her, and I certainly can't ask my father."

"Why not?" she asked.

"Gays know even less about men than women do. They just know about old movie stars and workout tips—and my father doesn't even know those! The last time he saw the inside of a gym was when Olivia Newton-John had that music video with the aerobics outfits."

Daisy was flummoxed. "You're making me nervous," she said, flipping the page in the *Daily Halo.* "Let's focus. Here—how about Helena Hears? Celebrity gossip will take your mind off the fact that you've become *completely hysterical.*"

Our favorite local drag queen, Helena Handcart, had recently started writing a gossip column for Halo City's record of ill repute. Neither one of us approved of Helena's affiliation with the raggiest newspaper in the city, but neither one of us could stop reading her column, either.

"Fine," I said, collapsing in my seat. "Read to me, Daisy. Soothe me."

"Ahem," she began. "Now, let's see here." She ran her finger down the page, looking for the good stuff. "Ha, this one's funny," she decided after a brief scan. "'Lisa Lincoln: Too Fat, Too Thin, *or both*?'"

"That's a first," I said.

"For real," Daisy agreed. "Listen to this: 'Buxom up-and-comer Lisa Lincoln, former star of the teen sitcom *She's with the Band!*, has sources atwitter with rumors that she may not be eating enough! Lovely Lisa, a notorious 'free spirit,' was spotted yesterday at the fashionable Deko Bistro munching on nothing but a skimpy-looking Caesar salad. Could Lisa be on a dangerous crash diet? For now, the jury's out. While it's true that Lisa's shoulder blades are looking mighty bony these days, the *Daily Halo*'s exclusive beach photos of La Lincoln reveal that her famously ample bottom remains as dimpled and rosy as the cheeks of a Campbell's soup kid. Which is it, Lisa—anorexic or *eat*-o-rexic? Whatever the case may be, it's no way for a role model to set an example for the young girls of America!"

Daisy turned the paper in my direction and made a gagging gesture. "Give me a break," she said.

I examined the photo of Lisa, standing in a bikini, with her backside to the camera.

"Her bottom looks fine to me," I said. "And is it just me, or is Helena Handcart a little bit harsh on the ladies?"

"There's irony for you," Daisy said. "But I guess if a drag queen's not allowed to be a body fascist, what's the world coming to?" She took the paper back and went on to the next item.

"'Speaking of curvy Lisa, we hear that the set of her latest fright fest, *Hell Circus*, has been less than peaceful. An inside source tells Helena Hears that security is tight. Why? Because a mysterious prankster is wreaking havoc on the set—and the main target of the misguided malevolence has been Ms. Lincoln herself! Just last week, La Lincoln's microscopic and much-adored teacup pooch, Bacteria, was kidnapped. Lisa returned to her deluxe double-wide trailer after a long day of shooting only to discover the dog's tragic disappearance. *Quelle horreur*, Lisa! Lucky for everyone, the dog was returned just a few days later, unharmed save for a nasty haircut. And keep this part on the DL because it's a secret: word has it that a shady character who calls himself "the Fox" is taking the so-called credit for this incident and others. What's going on at *Hell Circus*? Only time will tell. . . .'"

Daisy peered at me over the top of her shades. "Intriguing," she whispered, then returned to the tabloid. "'In other news from the *Hell Circus* set, here's a tasty blind item for those with an appetite for cat-fighting crones. It's true that the film has been the talk of Halo City since the stars arrived in town a few weeks ago. But what you might not know is that a certain Halo City expat recently joined the cast of the movie, replacing an old (and we mean really old) romantic adversary—under less than peachy circumstances. The has-been starlet in question arrived in HC just last week and headed straight to the Corona Beach set only hours after the previous occupant of her dressing room was given the hasty heave-ho. It wasn't the first time that "Icy Inga" snickety-snatched a prize out from under the nose of her rival, "Red Rita." Last time it happened was almost twenty years ago, when—'"

Abruptly Daisy trailed off.

"What?" I asked.

"Well, that was fun, wasn't it?" Daisy said with a phony smile. "I just love gossip, but it's getting hot out. Let's go to the supermarket and sit on the TV dinners in the freezer aisle!"

"Daisy," I warned. "You're not fooling me. Why did you stop reading?"

Daisy looked conflicted. "No reason!" she peeped.

I was unconvinced. "Read the rest of the item."

Daisy frowned. She knew it wasn't worth an argument. With an air of dismay she finished the article.

"'It wasn't the first time that "Icy Inga" snickety-snatched a prize out from under the nose of her rival, "Red Rita." Last time it happened was almost twenty years ago, when she stole "Rita's" man—and *married* him! The joke was on both of them, though. As it just so happened, the fellow in question prefers the company of other fellows! Now it's round two for these aging artistes. "Icy Inga" has won the battle, but who will win the war?'"

My stomach dropped as it all became clear.

Helena was talking about my mother. "Icy Inga" was Isabelle Dark.

I let the information sink in, twisting my hair around my pinky.

"Daisy," I said slowly.

Daisy furrowed her brow.

"I thought the point of reading the celebrity gossip was to get my mind *off* my problems."

Daisy scrunched her face into an expression of pained apology. "Sorry, Lulu. When I suggested that, you should have reminded me that your mother *is* a celebrity."

I stood and began gathering my things.

"Where are you going?" she asked.

"Duh," I said. "To Corona Beach. Hope you brought your bathing suit."

Daisy smiled. "I keep a bathing suit, a change of underpants, and a can opener on my person at all times for exactly this type of emergency."

"Ah," I said.

"You never know when you're going to need a can opener," Daisy said, sotto voce.

THREE

"CRAP!" I EXCLAIMED. "CRAP, crap, crap, crap, crap, crap!"

"That's no way for a lady to talk," Daisy scolded. "What's the matter?"

We were on the subway headed for Corona Beach, just settling in for the haul, when I realized what had slipped my mind: a certain boyfriend whose name rhymes with *gnarly* was supposed meet up with us at Little Edie's right about—I glanced at my watch—now.

"I can't believe I just forgot about him," I said. "He's going to be so pissed off."

"He'll understand," Daisy tried to reassure me. She didn't look convinced.

"Yeah, right," I said. Not only was I in for it with Charlie, but the news that Isabelle was in town hadn't put me in a great mood either.

I slouched back in my seat. "What is wrong with my mother? She didn't even tell me she was coming. When was she going to get in touch with me? Was she even going to call me?"

Daisy put her arm around my shoulders. "Oh, Lulu. I'm sure she was going to call you as soon as she got settled. It sounds like the whole thing was really last-minute."

"She's been here a week," I argued. "You'd think that would be enough time to pick up a phone."

Daisy shrugged sheepishly.

"Whatever," I said. "You've met my mother. You know how she is. I mean, I can't count the number of times I've been talking to her, thinking we're actually having a conversation, only to realize she's been running lines in her head from some movie she starred in twenty-five years ago."

About a decade before I was born, my mother had come close to being something like a movie star.

Back then, I'm told, every young, artsy, pretentious director under the sun was in love with her and wanted to cast her in his movies.

Isabelle's first starring role was in this British movie called *The Spiteful Heart.* In it she plays an American art student who goes to England and does all these things that don't make a whole lot of sense, looking very pensive all the while. In the final scene—the one she's still remembered for—Isabelle is standing by herself in a tiny rowboat, drifting off to sea. She's crying and hacking off her long, bleached hair in huge chunks, tossing it into the ocean as the sun sets.

And then, just before the credits roll, she shouts at the camera, "Goodbye, Britannia! Goodbye, O spiteful heart of mine! Hello, endless waters!"

Then it fades to black and you're like, *Um, what?*

What a dumb movie. But for some bizarre reason it was sort of a hit, and because of that, Isabelle was, briefly, kind of a big deal.

Then I was born.

Isabelle took some time off from the movie business to take care of me, and when she finally tried to get back into her career, it seemed that everyone had forgotten she existed. She went two years without a single part. Then one day Isabelle realized that she had a single, great, untapped talent: screaming at the top of her lungs.

Screeching, shrieking, squealing, whatever you want to call it— Isabelle was good at it. So there it was. With no other prospects, my mother's only choice was to resort to monster movies. It wasn't art, but at least she got to be in front of the camera—even if it was just to shake her boobs and caterwaul while some vampire, like, chopped off her head or whatever.

That lasted a good couple of years before Isabelle Dark, queen of screams, realized that she hated everything about her life. She just had to get out of Halo City and start over.

Isabelle left for good when I was almost ten. She and my dad had already been divorced for a while, thanks to the fact that he'd turned out to be a total homo, but it took my mother longer than she'd intended to actually pack up her things and move to Hollywood.

Truthfully, I barely noticed the difference once she was gone. Even when she *was* here in Halo City, I hardly saw her except for the few times that she needed me as a date for some premiere or awards ceremony or other photo opportunity.

I guess I should cut her a little slack. Of course, she'd been kind of depressed in those days, both about the "orientation" of her baby daddy and the drooping of her own legendary bosom. Still, is that an excuse to ignore your one and only daughter? She just checked out. No goodbye, no aloha; one minute she was my mother and the next minute she was just some quickly fading starlet who took me out to dinner every once in a while. At the time I remember thinking I saw her more in magazine photographs than I did in person, and after she decamped to Hollywood, that rule proved abiding.

In the last two years I haven't visited her more than three times. Our phone conversations, though slightly more frequent, are bizarre and circular—sort of like scenes from some weird foreign film.

Thank goodness I have my father. At least he and his boyfriend, Theo, *try* to act like parents. The same can't be said for Isabelle, whose behavior most closely resembles that of a dotty old aunt or, worse, the wacky upstairs neighbor on a third-string 1980s sitcom.

Still, I love her. Mostly because it's the rule. You have to love your mother. I think it even says that, like, in the Bible or something. I'm not very religious myself, and part of the reason is because God clearly left out a commandment that should have been really obvious: number eleven. *Love thy daughter.*

I was surprised to discover that I was kind of nervous when the train finally pulled into the Corona station. It was almost five o'clock, and the sun was starting to wane just slightly. Daisy and I stepped to the edge of the outdoor platform, a hundred feet above the street, where we paused to admire the view. From there, on the subway mezzanine, you can see all of Corona Beach. The gaudy, blinking Ferris wheel loomed in the distance, dwarfed only by a huge, creaky wooden roller coaster you couldn't pay me a trillion dollars to ride. Beyond that was the ocean.

"Should you call Charlie?" Daisy asked. "It's too bad he's not here. He loves thrill rides and all that."

"Yeah, I should," I said. But I didn't reach for my phone. I'd call him later, after I'd figured out exactly what was going on.

"Look!" Daisy pointed at the midway. It was lit up like a stadium, klieg lights everywhere. No mistaking it—that had to be the *Hell Circus* set.

Not far from the brightness, I could make out a long line of trailers, camped out in the street.

"There they are," I said. I took a deep breath.

"Don't sweat it, Lulu," Daisy said. She gave my arm an encouraging squeeze. "Your mother is going to be so happy to see you."

"If you say so," I said.

"Time to go swimming!" Daisy whipped off her caftan. I gawked. She had been wearing her bathing suit underneath the whole time.

"I told you I brought my bathing suit!" she said triumphantly.

"Where's the can opener?" I asked.

Daisy winked mischievously. "Sorry, Lulu, I can't tell you. A lady needs to keep some secrets." She pranced ahead of me and bounded down the stairs that led to the street. I couldn't quite muster the same enthusiasm. I was starting to wonder why I'd insisted on coming here in the first place.

I trailed behind Daisy until we could see the boardwalk. "Lulu!" She turned and scolded me. "Stop dawdling!"

"Maybe we should forget this," I called out.

"What are you talking about? It took us an hour to get here," Daisy shouted, marching back to meet me. "Lulu, please. What are you afraid of?"

"I don't know," I said. "That my mother won't remember my name, or that she'll have me thrown off the set, or that she'll just come right out and tell me that she wants me to stop bothering her altogether."

Daisy thought hard, considering the situation. "That's not going to happen," she finally said with conviction. "But if it does, I'll be here. We'll go home, have your father cook us a pot of spaghetti, and stay up all night watching Cinemax. And then at least you'll know for sure that your mother is a total creep in addition to being crazy."

"And that would be a good thing?" I asked.

She nodded gravely. "Better than not knowing. Dr. Phil says closure is v. v. important. Now let's go."

I shrugged. Fine. If Dr. Phil said so.

We knew we were in the right place when some hipster with a headset and a clipboard wouldn't let us go a step farther.

"I'm sorry," said the girl, a petite blonde with a severe blunt cut and little black tank top. "We're shooting a movie. You have to go around if you want to get to the roller coaster."

"I hate roller coasters," I said.

"Well, they hate you too," said the PA.

"I'm here to see my mother, Isabelle Dark."

"Who?" the PA asked.

"Isabelle Dark. She's in this movie, right?" I asked, suddenly feeling hopeful. Maybe we had misinterpreted the blind item and this was all a big mix-up.

The girl consulted her clipboard. "Oh, right. She's the *new* one. Playing the carnie queen. Hold on a sec." My heart sank. Not only *was* Isabelle in this movie; she was playing a carnie? This was certainly a new low.

The PA unclipped her walkie-talkie from her belt and consulted with the powers that be. Then she turned back to me and handed me a guest badge. "You can go ahead on to trailer four," she told me. "But the girl in the bikini has to wait. We've been having some security problems."

"Her name is Daisy," I said with my most withering stare. "And I'm sure my mother would like to see her too."

The girl with the clipboard didn't look impressed.

"Don't worry, Lulu." Daisy gave an impish smile. "I'll think of something to do."

She cantered off. I wondered what she had up her sleeve. Then I remembered she didn't have any sleeves. Oh, well. It was time to meet my mother.

I wandered through the set, knowing I really should call Charlie to let him know what was going on, but I just couldn't bring myself to do it.

What was he, my nanny? Why should I have to tell him where I was at all times?

The *Daily Halo* hadn't been lying about the tight security on the set. Everywhere I looked, there were guards talking into walkie-talkies and checking credentials. *Jeez,* I thought. *All this over some dumb dog.* I was just about to ask someone if they knew where Isabelle's trailer was when there was a commotion. I turned and caught sight of an older, redheaded woman, ranting loudly at a trio of unimpressed security guys.

"This is completely outrageous," the redhead was saying. "You people think you're important just because you have earpieces! Well, forgive me, but last time I checked, Lisa Lincoln was not Madame President, and you people were not secret service agents."

The guys had been humoring her, but their patience was clearly wearing thin. "I'm sorry, Ms. Greer," said the guard who I took for the leader. "It's time for you to go."

He grabbed hold of the redhead's elbow.

"I demand to speak to the director!" the redhead screeched. "Get me Fletcher Rose now!"

The security guard sighed, then spoke into his walkie-talkie. A moment later, a golf cart appeared and middle-aged man climbed out of the passenger seat.

"Fiona," the man addressed the redhead. "What seems to be the problem."

"Fletcher, these men will not let me onto the set," the redhead raved. "I have every right to be here. Tell these goons who I am. . . ."

Blah, blah, blah. I rolled my eyes to myself. That kind of behavior was just so LA.

I hurried away and was searching the midway for a sign of my mother when a pretty teenager in flats, designer sunglasses, and an empire-waist sundress came wandering by.

"Excuse me," I said to her. "Do you know where I could find a crazy blond actress—older, with enormous breasts and a devil-may-care disposition?"

She lowered her sunglasses and peered at me. Suddenly I recognized her.

"Lisa Lincoln!" I exclaimed, forgetting to act suave.

"That's me," she said flatly. "And you're Lulu Dark."

I was flabbergasted. Lisa Lincoln knew who *I* was?

"Um, yeah," I said blushing. "You've heard of me?"

"Duh," Lisa said. "Your mother. She's mentioned you. Mothers do that kind of thing."

"Oh. Uh, yeah, right," I stuttered, surprised. "She talks about you all the time too."

Lisa paused, regarding me for a moment. "Your mom's in the second trailer on the left, by the fun house." She turned to walk away.

"Wait!" I shouted after her. "I just wanted to say that I think your butt looks fine."

Lisa turned around. "What are you talking about?"

"You know," I said. "In Helena Hears this morning. They said you were anorexic and then they had that picture of you in the bikini and said that your butt was as dimpled as a Campbell's kid's cheeks. Don't pay attention to them; Helena's great, but she can be a little judgmental. And trust me, I'd hate to see the dimples on her butt."

Lisa gave me a wan sneer. "Thanks for the vote of confidence. You totally made my day." She swiveled again and stalked off.

"Wait!" I called. This time she ignored me.

Crap, I thought. I had done it again. A typical Lulu Dark moment. I try to be friendly and instead end up completely alienating a movie star. It was too bad, too—I wanted to ask her exactly what my mother had been saying about me.

Isabelle was waiting for me at the door to her trailer, looking as beautiful as ever but also unmistakably older than the last time I'd seen her. She was wearing ratty jeans and a white T-shirt, and her long, blond-white hair spilled down her back. She was just standing there, arm against the aluminum threshold.

"Lulu!" Isabelle exclaimed when she saw me approaching. "I'm so glad you made it. I was afraid you weren't going to call!"

"*I* wasn't going to call?" I said testily. "I didn't know you were in this movie. I didn't even know you were here,"

"I know! Crazy, isn't it?" she said, fluttering her hands about. "Come on in."

I followed her into the trailer.

Well, at least she had recognized me.

The inside of the trailer was cozy, messy, and not especially elaborate. There were a couch, a kitchenette, a dressing area, and a small TV. My mother's clothes were strewn everywhere.

"What's up, dear?" she said breezily, flopping onto the couch and crossing her legs in front of her Indian style. Her eyes darted around the trailer. She drummed her fingertips on her knee. For some reason, Isabelle seemed about as nervous as I felt.

I looked around for someplace to sit and finally settled on a bar stool at the vanity.

"I dunno," I said, swiveling my seat. "I just came to say hello. I mean, I read you were here in the *Daily Halo*! In a blind gossip item!"

"I was in Helena Hears?" Isabelle's eyes brightened. "What did it say?"

I glared at her, my annoyance bubbling up again.

"Oh, Lulu," Isabelle said, standing up. "Give me a hug." She stood up, walked over to me on my stool, and wrapped me in her arms. I stiffened. My nose was right in her cleavage.

"You don't even know how much I miss you," she cooed, swaying me back and forth in the grip of her embrace.

"Well, thanks," I said, still talking into her boobs. "I miss you too." But it sounded more like, "Mshssmpppfmmffffmp."

After a few moments I began to realize that Isabelle wasn't letting me go. I wriggled to extract myself from her headlock. "Listen," I said when I was finally free. "I'm glad you missed me, but next time you're in town, could you make the teensiest effort to see me?"

Isabelle turned away and put her palm to her temple dramatically. It's no accident that she's an actress.

"Lulu, I said I was sorry." She sighed.

I didn't bother to point out that no, actually, she hadn't said that, but whatever.

"It's been a crazy month," she continued. "I was going to—"

"Forget it," I said, cutting her off. "So how long are you in town?"

"I'm really not sure," Isabelle said, strolling over to the refrigerator. "You know me. I barely know where I am right now, much less where I'm going to be tomorrow. But I *do* know that I have to be in makeup in a few minutes. They're transforming me into a beautiful grande dame of the carnival. Busy, busy, busy, darling!"

"Well, do you want to do something while you're here? Should we have—I don't know—like, some mother-daughter time?"

I wasn't quite sure what mother-daughter time actually was, but I knew that Svenska was always desperate for more of it. Was there bra shopping involved? That seemed like a safe bet. Whatever it meant, I got the impression it was something that no mother, even a crappy absentee one, could turn down.

It seemed like the parental equivalent of challenging a cowboy to a shoot-out. A proposition that couldn't be brushed off.

Isabelle bit.

"Mother-daughter time!" she squealed. "That sounds fabulous! What say we meet up for cocktails later tonight? Just us girls. My friend Lisa showed me the charmingest spot yesterday. Do you have a pen?"

I closed my eyes, inhaled deeply, and counted to five. Isabelle really tries my patience. "I'm too young for cocktails," I reminded her. "I'm also too young to vote, just in case that was your backup plan."

"You are too funny!" Isabelle said. She twirled her hands in the air in a flamenco approximation and did a little pirouette across the floor. "Do people always tell you how funny you are? I bet they do."

I tried my best to ignore Isabelle's absurd, overly wound-up behavior. "Maybe we should just meet up for pastries. How about that?"

"Sounds wonderful. *Wonderful!*" Isabelle said. "Tonight at ten, say?"

"Fine," I said. "Two Moons Bakery on Peach Street. Don't be late."

"I shan't, Lu," Isabelle said. "Don't worry. I would never let you down."

"Uh-huh," I said. I held back a laugh. I was dubious, but all in all, it hadn't gone as badly with my mother as I'd been afraid it might. I blew her a kiss and left the trailer.

It was beautiful outside, my favorite time of day. The light had that golden, summery quality to it, the kind that only lasts for an hour or two before the sun sets. There was a mild breeze blowing in from the ocean. Everywhere movie people were scurrying around, doing whatever it is people do on a movie set.

Then I remembered: I had to find Daisy.

This was a task that was easier said than done. Daisy, worried about brain tumors, had recently thrown out her cell phone. And though she claimed to enjoy not having a phone ("It makes me feel like Laura Ingalls Wilder!" she was known to say), she was oblivious to the fact that it was a total pain for her friends, who had to rely on tin cans, twine, and ESP to stay in touch with her.

I was casting about, searching for her, when I felt a tap on my shoulder. I jumped with a start and whirled around.

"Hey," Daisy said.

ESP, apparently, works best every time.

"You scared me!" I laughed. "And how'd you get in here?"

Daisy reached into her cleavage and pulled out a pass that said SECURITY in big black letters.

"How did you get that?" I squealed.

She just smiled mysteriously. "I have my ways."

I threaded my arm through Daisy's. "Well," I said. "Let's get out of here before your *ways* get us into too much trouble."

Daisy looked at me like I'd lost it. "We have a *security* badge," she said. "Consider the possibilities."

"Another time," I said. "I got what I came for."

"Fine, then, be that way," she muttered, in her usual good humor.

We started to make for the train, but whoever was in charge of cosmic happenstance must have been favoring Daisy that day, because at that very moment, we heard an ear-shattering scream.

"What was that?" Daisy asked, a glint of excitement in her eyes.

"Nothing that concerns us, I'm sure," I said.

It wasn't Isabelle, I knew. Her scream is patented, and that wasn't it.

Daisy tugged at my arm. "Come *on*, Lulu, don't be a spoilsport."

I didn't say anything, but I let her drag me toward the sound of the screaming. It wasn't too hard to figure out where it was coming from; everyone on the set seemed to be racing in the same direction, so just we followed them. When we arrived at the epicenter of the hubbub, we found Lisa Lincoln crouched on the ground outside an enormous trailer, breathing heavily into a brown paper lunch sack while a bevy of handlers tried to comfort her. The door to the trailer stood open, and several suit-clad guards were hovering.

"What's going on?" Daisy asked me.

"I'm not sure," I said, my curiosity piqued. I slunk closer to Lisa's entourage. In the confusion I was only able to pick up snatches of their conversation—"security breach," "prank," and "the Fox."

I turned to Daisy. "Give me that pass of yours."

Daisy handed it over, and I marched up the steps of the trailer, waving it in front of myself with an air of importance. One secret I had learned during my stint as a "teen detective": you can get away with a lot as long as you display a certain amount of confidence.

"Excuse me!" I said, scrunching past the guys at the door. "Coming through! I need to take a look!" Nobody stopped me.

I stepped inside the trailer and my heart sank. This was more than a prank. It was your standard, by-the-numbers, the-worst-is-yet-to-come gesture, familiar to anyone who has even a passing familiarity with cheap paperbacks.

La Lincoln's trailer had been completely demolished. Her clothes were strewn everywhere, shredded like confetti, and what seemed like a million pink throw pillows had all been slashed. Feathers were drifting through the air. And scrawled across the wall, in black Sharpie, was the phrase *Beware the Fox.*

I had to roll my eyes. Dramatic much?

Without even thinking about it, I whipped my trusty little digital camera from my handbag and began snapping away. You never know when photos of the evidence are going to come in handy.

Not that I was in any way interested in solving this mystery, I reminded myself. Mysteries do not interest me in the least. Not this summer. Still . . .

Graffiti: *click.*

Slashed clothes: *click.*

Overturned dresser: *click.*

I gasped as a meaty hand closed around the back of my neck. I whirled around and found a giant man in a black suit glaring at me.

"What do you think you're doing?" he asked. His voice rumbled, so low that it probably registered on the Richter scale.

"Um . . ." I searched my repertoire of excuses and came up empty. "Nothing?" I suggested.

"Nice try," said the goon. "Come with me." He grabbed me by the shoulders and steered me toward the door.

Frankly, I wasn't in the mood to be manhandled.

"Sorry!" I yelped. I ducked to my hands and knees and began crawling madly for the exit. The goon hadn't been expecting the move. He lunged for me, but he was too slow. I had already escaped to the outside, where I rose to my feet and began to run. Daisy, always at the ready, didn't need to be told to follow.

"What happened?" she shouted, hot on my heels. "What did you see in there?"

"Remember that item in Helena Hears?" I wheezed. "Well, someone really *is* out to get Lisa Lincoln. The Fox has struck again!"

"Oh my gosh!" Daisy exclaimed. "So what's our next move? Are we going to find out who the Fox really is?"

"No!" I squealed. "This thing with the Fox may be a mystery, but it's not our mystery. We are not getting involved."

"Sure, we aren't," Daisy said. She failed to conceal her smirk.

Later that night I sat alone in the café on Peach Street, waiting for my mother to arrive. I was on time. Naturally, she was not.

I'd ordered a slice of chocolate cake and I was sitting by myself at a table, drinking a cappuccino while I waited. The later it got, the more I started to stew. Isabelle had promised that she would be on time. Isn't that what "I shan't, Lu, I would never let you down" means? And why did she have to say stupid things like that in the first place?

At ten thirty, when she *still* hadn't rolled in, I called her phone.

I knew it was basically pointless. I couldn't even remember the last time that Isabelle Dark actually answered her cell phone, but whatever. Whatever. *What. Ever.*

Naturally, Mom's voice mail picked up. "It's Isabelle Dark. Leave me a message unless we've had carnal relations in the past five years, in which case you can hang up now."

And then a beep. I groaned and just hung up.

I glanced around the café. Everyone else looked so happy. There were couples on dates, snuggling and flirting and leaning into each other. Friends sharing tremendous desserts with multiple forks.

I felt like a total loser—a lonely girl sitting by herself, pushing her chocolate cake around her plate. I guess it could have been my imagination, but I got the distinct impression that everyone was looking at me, wondering what my deal was.

I was right about at least one person. The waitress, a tattooed dark-haired girl in her twenties, noticed my unease and sidled over to me.

"Boys can total asses, huh?" she said charitably.

"Not boys," I replied. "Mothers."

Her eyes widened. "Wow. Your *mother* stood you up? That *is* bad."

"She'll be here eventually," I said, sitting up straighter. "She's just making me sweat."

The waitress nodded. "Yeah. I'm sure she'll be here soon."

An hour later that same waitress brought me a vanilla latte on the house. A pity latte, I realized. I was grateful, but for some reason, I couldn't swallow it down. It tasted a little bitter. Maybe the milk was sour.

Around midnight I figured it was a lost cause. I grabbed my purse and left the café. By myself.

FOUR

THE NEXT DAY I WOKE, WITH a raging headache, to the sound of banging at my door. I rolled over and looked at the clock. It was only noon.

"What?!" I yelled.

"Wake up, Lu," my father's voice called from the other side of the door. "Charlie's here!"

Ugh. Just what I needed. "Tell him I'm having my period!" I called. It was the only excuse I could think of.

My father sounded surprised. "Um, okay. I'll tell him that."

"Never mind," I grumbled. "I'll be out in a minute."

Groggily, I rose to my feet and pulled on a white tank top and a pair of sweatpants. I slipped on my glasses. Well, at least now I could see.

Charlie was sitting at the breakfast table with my father and his boyfriend, Theo, eating a bowl of cereal and watching a talk show.

"Oh no, she didn't!" some woman on the screen was screaming.

"Oh yes, she did!" another woman screamed.

Charlie gave me a meaningful, hangdog look. I tried not to roll my eyes.

"Charlie says you stood him up yesterday," Theo said.

"Oh no, she *didn't*!" said my father.

"Oh yes, she *did*!" Theo said.

I, on the other hand, sighed deeply. Sometimes I find Dad and Theo's extreme gayness endearing. Other times I find it tiresome. This was one of the tiresome times.

"Butt out," I said. "I'm grumpy." I still hadn't told them about what had happened with Isabelle, and to be honest, it wasn't something I felt like sharing.

So we all just stood there, looking at each other, while my blood pressure started to rise.

This was so inappropriate of Charlie, showing up like this unannounced. He got away with it because he knows Dad thinks it's funny to torment me. He likes the way Charlie "keeps me on my toes." Whatever *that* means.

I jerked my chin at Charlie. "Come talk to me in my room," I said. He stood up and followed me. Like a puppy.

"No smooching!" my father called after us.

"Grow up!" I retorted.

I closed the bedroom door and turned to face my boyfriend. He was still making that woe-is-me face. Truthfully, it was kind of cute. He was wearing tight, frayed pea green corduroys and a vintage Stevie Nicks T-shirt. His hair was falling in his eyes. He looked good.

"Fine. I'm sorry!" I said. "It was a total accident!"

"Uh-huh," he said.

"Listen, there were extenuating circumstances. *Isabelle* is in town."

"What?" Charlie looked surprised. "Isabelle, your mother?"

"That's the one," I said. "And she didn't even tell me she was coming. I read about it in the *newspaper*."

"Wow," said Charlie.

"I was so shocked that it slipped my mind I was supposed to meet you," I fibbed. "*Now* do you understand?"

Charlie's sourness broke. "Of course I do. Oh, Lulu." He reached out, pulled me close, and planted one—right on my lips.

I melted into him. He tasted slightly like grapefruit. It was nice. For a minute. Then that minute was over and he kept on kissing me.

I pulled away. "What are you doing?"

"Kissing you." He frowned, confused.

"Well, stop," I said.

"But why—?" he began.

"Because I'm upset," I interrupted him. "I'm not in the mood for a round of seven minutes in heaven."

Charlie looked chagrined. "Oh. Okay. I'm sorry."

I gritted my teeth. Why did he always have to be so . . . so *sorry* all the time?

I grabbed my favorite new T-shirt and a pair of jogging shorts from the top of my dresser and escaped behind my vintage dressing screen.

"I have to go now," I called as I slipped out of my pj's.

"Where?" Charlie asked.

"I have to find my mom," I said, pulling the T-shirt over my head. "We had a date last night and she didn't show."

"Oh," Charlie said. "Okay. Let's go."

"No. I have to go by myself," I told him, tying the drawstring at my waist.

"Why?" he asked again.

I stepped out from behind the screen. "Just because," I said.

Because you've become a weird love-zombie! I thought.

Charlie just looked at me. He didn't say anything. I felt a tiny pang in my heart. But maybe it was just that I needed a bagel.

Enough of that. I grabbed my bag and booked it.

"Lulu!" I heard my father call as I slammed the door to the apartment behind me. I felt bad, ignoring him. I just knew that I had to be by myself. I headed for the subway. I took the long route.

Walking through the winding, tree-lined streets of my neighborhood, Halo Village, I wondered about certain things. Things like: What was wrong with my mother? And: Didn't Charlie think that sporting a Stevie Nicks T-shirt, even ironically, was a little bit sissyish? And finally: Why was I being such a fishwife? Did I get it from my mom?

That was the last thing: Mom. Where was she, anyway? I supposed that she might still be shooting at Corona Beach, but I didn't want to risk the hour-long train ride there only to find that she was gone.

I dialed Isabelle's cell, and again there was no answer. I didn't bother leaving a message.

I sat down on a bench, annoyed and frustrated. What now?

Here's a piece of advice: When at a crossroads, apply ChapStick.

ChapStick is, like, the great clarifier. I whipped out a tube of eucalyptus and smeared on a fresh coat. I think it was the smell that did it. A thought occurred to me.

I flipped open my cell phone again and scanned through the list of names until I got to *H. Helena Handcart.* I called her up.

Helena picked up after one ring.

Helena is a very substantial lady. In a world full of unreliable mothers, it's good to have four-hundred-pound cross-dressers around when you need them.

"Lulu!" came the booming falsetto on the line. "How's the family reunion going? Are you and mom having fun yet?"

"Not quite," I admitted. "How come you didn't tell me she was here?"

"It didn't occur to me that you didn't know," Helena said. "I mean, she's *your* mother."

"That's the theory, at least." I sighed.

"Oh, little goose, don't be so gloomy," Helena said. "All's well that ends well, right? Speaking of which, I sincerely hope that you're going to turn over your exclusive crime scene photographs from Lisa's trailer yesterday."

I blinked. "Wait—how do you know about that?"

"I have my sources." Helena laughed.

"Right." I stood up straighter. "That's exactly why I'm calling. Do you know where my mother is today? She stood me up last night."

"I have no idea," Helena cooed. "Why don't you just call her?"

"She's not a cell phone kind of girl," I said.

"Well." Helena paused for effect. I could tell she was slipping into boldface type. "I'm sorry, but I haven't heard anything about her whereabouts today. Yesterday was her last day shooting, you know."

"What?" I yelped.

"Her part was pretty small. The whole brouhaha about her replacement was a lot of fuss about nothing, if you ask me."

"She didn't tell me she was done," I said.

I couldn't believe it. Had she headed back to LA? Without even saying goodbye?

"I don't know what to tell you, Lulu," Helena said. "I'll see what I can find out if you want."

"Sure, Helena," I said.

I hung up, dejected, and headed for Little Edie's to drown my sorrows in a cup of coffee and a scone.

That night, dad took me out to his favorite Chinese restaurant, Gang of Four, right around the corner from our apartment.

"What's wrong, Lu?" he asked, on the way there. "Ever since you ran out of the house this morning, you've been acting like someone spiked your coffee with a triple-dose of Klonopin."

I let it all spill out. Well, the stuff about Isabelle, at least. I left out most of the business with Charlie. My father listened intently, not interrupting. When I was done, he wrapped his arm around my waist. We walked down the street, in the gathering humidity, to the restaurant. I was glad he was my father.

"Your mom is a very complicated lady," my dad told me, after the waiter took our order—a pupu platter, to split.

"Yeah, about as complicated as a game of tic-tac-toe," I sneered. "And just as pointless, too."

"I'm being serious, Lulu," my father said. "Don't confuse being clever with being a snip. It's not charming."

"Fine," I sniffed. Dad nodded, futzing with his chopsticks.

I looked at him. I wanted to ask him something.

"Why did you marry her?" It was something I had been wondering for, I don't know, like my whole life at the very least. He looked surprised at the question, which just goes to show how clueless he can be about certain things that should be so incredibly obvious.

"I was in love with her," he told me.

"Why were you in love with her?" I asked. "Because I, for one, would really like to know the reason."

"If you had known her then, you wouldn't wonder," he said. "Anybody would have been in love with her. She was the kind of girl you fall in love with. She was a lot like you, you know." He paused registering the horror on my face.

People like you aren't supposed to fall in love with ladies, I wanted to say. But I didn't. I knew he wouldn't have a reasonable response anyway.

"You're a lot more sensible, of course," he added.

I examined the chips in my nail polish and prayed for the food to arrive.

When it finally did, the waiter lit up the gas flame in the middle of the serving tray, and dad and I each skewered up a piece of teriyaki.

"What you need to know about Isabelle," my father said, "is that she is trying."

"I've never gotten the slightest impression that that's the case," I said.

"She loves you," he said. "She really, really does."

"She sure doesn't act like it."

"I know," my father said. "But don't blame her for everything. I deserve some of the blame too. Parents aren't perfect. Even me."

I had to laugh at that. "I don't think anyone suggested that you were."

Dad looked slightly hurt. "But you're good enough, as far as things go, I guess," I said. He smiled.

"Well, maybe I am and maybe I'm not," he said. "But Isabelle wouldn't be the way she is now if it weren't for me. You know that, right? It's not really fair that I get to be the good guy when I'm just as responsible as she is for . . . everything. If not more."

Things were getting very uncomfortable. This conversation had been a long time coming, but it had snuck up on me. I picked a piece of beef from my front teeth with my pinky nail.

"You mean because of how you turned into a homo and dumped her like last week's moldy macaroni casserole?" I said, taking even myself aback.

Dad winced. "That's one very hurtful way of putting it."

"Sorry. But why *did* you do that, anyway?" I asked.

He shrugged. "I don't know why, Lulu. I wanted to be happy, I guess. If I had stayed with your mother, all three of us would have been unhappy."

"Do you wish you hadn't married her?" I asked.

"No," my father said. "Then I never would have had you." He paused, chewing on his food, and thought for a moment. "That's the main reason," he went on. "But not the only one. I'm very glad for the time I had with your mother. It was important."

"Do you think she feels the same way?" I asked.

"I think it's more complicated for her," he said.

I looked down. The food was almost gone. There were little beads of sweat forming a centimeter above my father's eyebrows, even though we were sitting right under the air-conditioning vent, and I knew that even though he was trying to play it cool, he was feeling just as weird as I was about our line of convo. "Let's change the subject," I said.

"If you want to," said my father, clearly relieved. "What do you want to talk about?" He took a nervous sip of his water.

I applied a coat of ChapStick, racking my brain for any other topic at all.

"I saw the craziest reality television show the other night," I said. "You should totally watch it when it comes on again. Actually, Theo would love it most of all. It was called *Who Wants to Marry My Pomeranian.* You would not believe the outfits they made these people wear."

My dad laughed so hard he shot water out of his nose, across the table. So much for that last piece of shrimp.

After we'd paid the bill, Dad and I parted ways with a hug in front of the restaurant. He was meeting Theo at a gallery downtown for an opening. I walked home by myself, thinking about what we'd talked about.

Was my father right, or was he just beating up on himself, I wondered? In the end, I decided that it was a little of both. I couldn't blame

Isabelle for being upset about the way things had gone down. But at a certain point, enough is enough. At a certain point, a grown-ass lady needs to get over it and remember that she has responsibilities—most of all to her child, but not least of all to herself.

Halfway down the block from the apartment there was a crowd of scruffy-looking guys gathered practically on my doorstep. As I drew closer, I realized that they were clustered around a black town car that was idling in the street, blocking a fire hydrant. Stationed next to the car was an enormous, Amazonian-looking woman in a formfitting black suit. Her blond hair was cropped close; her hands were folded behind her back, elbows akimbo. She was just standing there, stone-faced, while the guys, all of whom were clutching cameras, stood around chatting with each other. They started to perk up as they noticed my approach, but none of them made a move to do anything.

"What's going on?" I wondered aloud when I was within speaking distance of the throng.

"Lulu Dark," the blond woman said in a firm, imposing voice.

It wasn't a greeting and it wasn't a question. It was more like a command. She was scary looking, but I was curious.

"Yeah. What's up?" I asked, stepping closer.

She kept her hands behind her back and gestured with a nod. "Get in the car."

I stared the woman in the eye. "I don't normally get into a stranger's town car without a very fine reason," I told her.

"I'm Trish Archer. I'm Lisa Lincoln's bodyguard," she replied, not

moving a muscle. "I believe you know Lisa. She's in the car and she'd
like to speak with you. It's important."

I was intrigued. Lisa Lincoln was a real, bona fide movie star. I
was just . . . Lulu. Why would she go to this much trouble to see me?

I nodded to Trish. She opened the car door and stepped aside.
Taking a deep breath, I slid in.

And there, sitting stiffly on a plush leather seat in all her resplen-
dency, was Lisa Lincoln. She was sucking on a lollipop, and the smell
of sour apple wafted through the car.

At her side was a tiny dog, shaved to its bare skin except for a
long plume of fur that ran from his forehead down his back, like a
doggie Mohawk.

The famous and recently maligned Bacteria, I presumed.

Lisa looked as beautiful and busty as ever, which led me to wonder: Did this girl ever go anywhere without a full face of makeup and
her hair blown out like she'd just stepped off the cover of *Teen People*?

"Fancy running into you like this, Lisa," I deadpanned. I tried to
give Bacteria a pat, but he just bared his teeth and snarled.

"Like master, like doggie," I remarked.

I guess I was still a bit annoyed with Lisa for her snooty behavior
of yesterday afternoon, but there's just something about famous
people. You can't help but be drawn under their spell. I guess that's
why they're famous.

Today Lisa had a haunted air about her. She bit down hard on
her lollipop and blew a nervous bubble with the gum that had been
encased inside.

"Lulu," she said.

"Lisa," I said, mocking her just a little.

"I have bad news," she said.

I groaned inwardly. I knew where this was going.

"Is this about your little prankster?" I asked. "The one who keeps vandalizing your things? Because I don't know what my mother told you, but I'm really not into solving mysteries these days."

Lisa stared at me intently. "You might change your mind when I tell you the latest wrinkle. Your mother has disappeared."

FIVE MY MOTHER? DISAPPEARED?

I sat quietly for a moment, taking it all in.

"This is so typical of her," I said finally. "What a drama queen."

Lisa dropped her phlegmatic affect.

"That's all you have to say? What is *wrong* with you?" she snapped. "I tell you your own mother's been kidnapped and you act like you just broke a nail?"

I rolled my eyes. "Isabelle is just making some kind of scene. People don't get *kidnapped*."

"Yes, they do," Trish Archer said.

I whirled around in surprise. I'd totally forgotten that she was with us in the first place. I guess the ability to blend seamlessly into new leather interiors was part of her job description.

"If people didn't get kidnapped all the time, I wouldn't have a job," Trish said. "You just don't hear about it. It gets"—she put her index finger to her lips—"hushed up."

"Poor little Bacteria got kidnapped just last week," Lisa pointed out. And Bacteria, as if on cue, looked up at me and whined dolefully.

Regardless, I was unmoved. "I hate to break this to you, Lisa, but my mother is an incorrigible flake. She's probably out at the discotheque as we speak."

"You don't believe me," Lisa said, mostly to herself. She pressed a button on her armrest and rolled down the privacy barrier that separated us from the driver. "Sam," she called up to the front seat. "Take us to the hotel, please."

She rolled the window back up and turned to me. "Fine. *You're* the girl detective. If you want evidence, I've got it."

I bristled. If there was one thing I didn't like, it was being called a girl detective. My thoughts on that subject are very well documented. But I kept my irritation to myself.

I was convinced that there was nothing to be concerned about. Still, it would be cool to see what Lisa Lincoln's hotel room was like.

As the car sped uptown, I pressed my face against the window. Halo City was lit up like a video game. It was beautiful. I imagined that I was a pinball, bouncing through the streets, racking up points with every passing moment. Maybe I'd had a bad day. But at least life was, like, *happening*.

"You act like you haven't lived here for the last seventeen years," Lisa said.

"It never gets old," I told her, taking my eyes off the vista. "Superman can keep Metropolis. I'll take Halo City."

"Well, it sure beats Hollywood," Lisa said. She blew a bubble gum bubble and then popped it. She seemed to be considering something.

"How did you find out where I live, anyway?" I wondered suddenly.

"I called Charlie," she said.

I nearly swallowed my tongue. "Charlie? Charlie *Reed*? How do you know him?"

"Your mother mentioned him. I think it's sweet the way you guys have been friends since forever."

"Oh," I said. But I thought it was weird. "How did you get his phone number?"

Lisa gave me a mischievous glance. "When a young starlet wants to get in touch with Halo City's richest high school teenager, it usually isn't a problem."

I stared at Lisa.

Huh. So the movie star who put the *b* in *buxom* had Charlie's phone number. That was . . . fine, I guessed.

"Listen, I didn't mean to be a bitch yesterday afternoon," Lisa told me, registering my uneasiness as something else. "Sorry about that. I was just jealous."

"You? Jealous of me?" I was incredulous. This was *Lisa Lincoln* we were talking about. What did I have that she could possibly want?

"I dunno," she said. "You just seem like you have a great life. You're always running around having adventures. You live in this awesome place. You've got, like, an amazing boyfriend and the world's coolest mom. I mean, assuming you're right and she's not, you know, kidnapped or whatever. Think about it, Lulu. You've got it made."

I would have been less flabbergasted if she'd pulled her eyeballs out of her head and juggled them.

"You think *my* mom is cool," I said, making sure I had heard right.

Lisa nodded. "She's been so nice to me. And I never met my real mom, you know. Isabelle's the closest I've got. I just hope she's okay."

I shook my head, disbelieving. "Does my mother have a clone or something?"

Lisa searched me with her disarmingly blue eyes. "She said you guys had some problems. But you should give her another chance. I don't know what I would have done without Isabelle. Most actresses are backstabbing phonies. In fact, everyone in LA is pretty much a total ass hat. But your mom totally took me under her wing. She makes being in the movie business almost bearable."

"Ha! That's a laugh!" I hooted. "Hoo! What a laugh!"

Even to my own ears my words sounded a little stilted, but I couldn't let Lisa see how hurt I was. All this time Isabelle had been nurturing a relationship with a surrogate daughter rather than the one she'd actually given birth to.

Lisa cocked her head and raised an eyebrow at me. She opened her mouth and was about to say something when the car slowed to a halt.

"Here we are," said Lisa, squinting to see out the tinted window. She spit her gum into the ashtray and fumbled in her purse. All of a sudden I detected a trace of franticness about her.

"Want some makeup?" she asked, not looking up.

"No, thank you," I said.

"Suit yourself." Lisa shrugged. She glanced at me briefly and smiled like a sphinx, then opened her compact and began powdering her face with speedy expertise. "How do I look?" she asked me after about thirty seconds of lightning-quick artistry.

"Um, gorgeous like always?" Did this person not realize that she didn't need to wear all that foundation?

Lisa turned to Trish. "How do I look?" she asked.

"A little more eye shadow," the bodyguard suggested. Lisa complied and then turned to me.

"Are you ready?"

"Well, we're here, aren't we?" God. Why was Lisa being so neurotic all of a sudden?

"Here we go, then," she said. "Don't forget to turn it on, Lulu!"

Trish popped open the car door and stepped out. There was screaming. A trillion lights started flashing. Suddenly I realized what was going on—but it was too late. Lisa took a deep breath and grabbed my hand.

"Oh no you don't!" I said, pulling in the other direction.

"No time for regrets, Lulu," Lisa said. "Just work it!"

And suddenly it was like she had become a different person: calm, composed, and—above all—*famous*.

She stuck a long, tan leg out of the car onto the street and followed it gracefully, pulling me with her against my deepest protests.

Before I knew it, I found myself caught in a flurry of snapping flashbulbs and shouting.

"Lisa, over here!"

"Give me a good one, Lisa!"

"You're beautiful, Lisa!"

"Lisa, who's your friend?"

There I was, in my sweatpants, in the middle of a full-blown paparazzi attack. Why hadn't I taken Lisa up on the makeup?

I felt terrified—I mean, I was paralyzed, no exaggeration. Lisa, on the other hand, was in her element. She waved and turned and laughed, and waved and turned and laughed, and tossed her hair playfully, and waved and laughed some more, all the while gripping my hand tightly.

"Work it, Lulu," she hissed through a grin of steel. "You're gonna be on the front page tomorrow whether you like it or not."

What would Isabelle do? I thought. Bizarrely, the thought of my mother helped. All I had to do was pretend I was her and I was okay. I winked and tilted my head into Lisa's, pouting my lips a little to disguise the fact that I barely have any, really. I put a hand on my hip and extended a sweatpant-clad leg.

"There you go," Lisa whispered. "Other way now." Seamlessly we turned in the other direction and repeated the same move. I giggled a little. I could get used to this.

"Thanks, guys," Lisa said breezily to the photographers, and we were done. Just like that, the mask came off, and she trotted through the crowd up to the front of the Halo Grand, with me following at her heels.

"God," she said. "What a pain."

Wait—what? "It seemed to me that you liked it," I told her.

"I'm good at my job," she told me. "But it's still a job."

We strode through the lobby of the hotel. Lisa either didn't notice or pretended not to notice the fact that every head in the room turned to stare at her as she passed. But as much as I tried to be cool, I couldn't ignore it. I could feel a huge, nervous smile spreading across my face—the kind of smile that pops up in the most inappropriate situations, like during funerals and health class with Mr. McDonald.

Going out with Isabelle had never, ever been like this. Sure, every now and then some creepy science-fiction fan would ask for her autograph, but in general she went pretty much unnoticed. This was something utterly . . . other.

"Come on," Lisa said. "Now you'll see what I'm talking about."

"I'll stay here in the lobby," Trish said, waving us on as we stepped into the elevator. I jumped. For the second time in an hour I'd forgotten she was with us.

"I could use a bodyguard." I sighed. "I'm always being tailed by someone or other."

The doors slid closed. We rode up to the thirtieth floor.

"I'm hoping you'll be able to use your uncanny powers of deduction to come up with an explanation for this one," Lisa said. She strolled down the hall to room 3011, removed the DO NOT DISTURB sign, and unlocked the door. "Voila. Isabelle's room."

"You have a key?" I asked.

"My room's right across the hall. She likes me to wake her up in the morning—you know what a heavy sleeper she is. She's always afraid she won't hear the wake-up call."

"Ah," I said.

I didn't remember my mother being a heavy sleeper. I didn't really know what kind of a sleeper she was. It had been a very long time since we had slept in the same place.

Inside, Isabelle's fancy-schmancy Ian Schrager–wanna-be room was littered with clothes. The bedsheets were lying on the floor. But that wasn't suspicious. One thing I *did* know about my mother was that she wasn't exactly a neat freak.

"The Mystery of the Slobby Starlet," I mused. "Or should we call it *The Clue in the Dirty Underpants*? This looks pretty normal to me. How long has she been gone?"

"Last time I saw her was around eight o'clock last night," Lisa said. "She was done with her part of the shoot, but she was going to stick around Halo City until I was done too."

"She'll be back later. I bet you anything."

"I'm not so sure. Look at this." Lisa led me over to the desk, where there was a neat stack of news clippings. I flipped through them. They were mostly gossip items, and they were all about the same thing: the Fox. They dated back several months, when the Fox had been just a rumor about a jealous ne'er-do-well trying to get revenge on young starlets.

"This doesn't mean anything," I said. "You already told me that Isabelle took an interest in you. This just means she was looking into whoever's been terrorizing you. And the only thing that's suspicious about that is the fact that she's worried about anything other than herself."

"You don't think it's a little weird?" Lisa asked.

Sure, it did seem a *little* weird, but certainly not weird enough to make me think that she had been kidnapped.

"Oh, I almost forgot," Lisa said. "There's something else." She pointed to the dresser.

"What?" I asked. The dresser was littered with jewelry, receipts, and piles of loose change. Again, nothing out of the ordinary.

"The picture's gone," Lisa pointed out.

"What picture?" I asked.

"The picture of you."

I waited for her to fill me in.

"Isabelle takes a picture of you wherever she goes. If it's gone, it means she's not coming back anytime soon. I'm sure of it. She must have managed to grab it before they could take her."

Okay, so I'm not going to lie. I was intrigued. "Which picture is it?" I asked.

"You're at the beach," Lisa said. "You must be, like, seven years old. You're wearing a green bathing suit and you're standing in the surf, with your arms over your head."

"I remember that picture," I said. Lisa just smiled.

Against my better judgment, I found that I was getting a little choked up. I swallowed hard, but a sound at the door busted up our moment. A key turning.

"Isabelle!" Lisa whispered.

I shook my head. "Shhh! Hurry! Under here!"

We fell to our knees and crawled under the bed just as the door opened.

Unfortunately, my instincts hadn't failed me. It wasn't Isabelle entering the room

"It's just housekeeping," Lisa hissed in my ear as two fortyish blond women in French maid outfits walked into the room. I squeezed her thigh, signaling her to keep quiet. These didn't look like any maids I'd ever seen. For one thing, their "uniforms" weren't conducive to actual housekeeping. The skirts were too short, the necklines too low. They seemed to have been purchased at a costume shop. For another, other than one pathetic-looking feather duster, they weren't carrying any kind of cleaning accoutrements.

And although I couldn't place their faces, these middle-aged maids looked strangely familiar.

The women made their way straight for the dresser.

"Here it is," the wrinklier one said.

"What an idiot, leaving this stuff behind for anyone to find," said the other. Her lips looked ready to burst from the collagen she'd had pumped into them.

And then they left. As soon as the door closed again, Lisa moved to scramble out from under the bed, but I held her back.

"Wait," I said. We lay scrunched there for a few more minutes until we were satisfied that the coast was clear and then emerged from our hiding spot.

"Well." I sighed. "The only way that could have been any more suspicious is if Professor Plum had marched in here and hit us over the head with a candlestick."

Lisa looked nervous. I was rattled, but I was also completely exhausted.

"I have to give it to you, Lisa," I said. "You were on to something after all."

"Who do you think they were?" Lisa asked.

"Cleanup crew," I said. "They were removing the evidence."

"What are we going to do?"

"I don't know what you're going to do, but I'm going to go home and think about all of this," I told her. "I'll figure out my next move. What about you? Are you shooting all day?"

"Yeah," Lisa said. She checked her watch. "Jesus. My call's in five hours. I'm going to look like hell. Just watch, all the columns are going to say I was out late drinking. 'Lisa's Wild Night.'" She shook her head ruefully. "I could write the headline myself."

"You didn't recognize those cleaning ladies, by any chance?" I asked as we headed back out into the hall.

Lisa scrunched her face up in thought. "I dunno," she said. "Practically every woman I know over the age of forty looks like that. Blond. Booby. Lips like hot dogs and a face pulled so tight you can practically see through the skin. It's hard to say. Why?"

"I dunno," I said. "There was just something about them."

She walked me to the elevator, where Trish was still waiting.

"Hey, Trish," Lisa said. "Did you notice anyone funny? Some weird-looking cleaning ladies?"

"Nope," Trish replied.

I rolled my eyes. Some bodyguard.

Lisa pulled out her cell phone. "I'll have Sam drive you home," she said. "Call me tomorrow."

I nodded.

On the ride home I pondered what we had seen. And a depressing thought occurred to me. Lisa was operating under the assumption that the Fox had left those clippings behind when he (or she?) kidnapped my mother.

But another scenario seemed much more likely to me.

The Fox left those clippings . . . because it was her room.

Or to put it another way, what if the Fox *was* Isabelle Dark?

SIX "BREAKFAST, LULU!" THEO CALLED.

I groaned.

Let me make a proclamation. I, Lulu Dark, am lazy. If there's one thing in the world that I hate, it's getting out of bed. I'm not ashamed of it, either.

Say it loud: I'm idle and proud.

I am snoozing: hear me snore.

I'm here-y, I'm weary; get used to it!

On the other hand, as indolent as I may be, I also like to eat. And I like my food served hot. I had a choice to make. I could keep sleeping, but if I stayed in bed all day, I would miss Theo's breakfast. He's a very good cook.

"Coming!" I shouted.

When I crawled out of my room, Dad and Theo were sitting at the breakfast table, grinning impishly at me over a huge platter of pancakes, a frittata, and a pitcher of mimosas.

"What?" I asked. "Why are you looking at me like that?"

Then I glanced down at my plate. Sitting next to it was a copy of the *Daily Halo*, with the following screaming headline:

LA LINCOLN'S WILD NIGHT!!

And there I was in the half-page photograph, clutching Lisa's arm, my eyes half closed and my mouth twisted into a disgusting Daffy Duck grimace.

"Oh God!" I whined.

"You're famous!" said Theo.

"I can't believe this!" I said. "I look like I just huffed a can of Reddi-wip!"

"You look fine," my father said. "Beautiful, even."

"Thanks for trying," I said.

"Have you thought about practicing your expressions in the mirror?" Theo suggested. "That's what those girls on *Next Top Model* always do. Sometimes it even helps."

I gave him a glare that said, *Shut it*, then sat down, helped myself to a heaping pile of food, and filled them in on the events of the previous day.

"Weird," said my father.

"Very weird," Theo agreed.

"What do you think I should do?" I asked.

"Call Jaycee," my father said. "I bet she knows what's going on. It must all be some kind of misunderstanding."

Jaycee Frost is my mother's constantly beleaguered agent. Dad was right. She probably *would* have an explanation. It was just too bizarre to think that there wasn't one.

So after I was done eating, I called the agency. It was no dice, though. Jaycee was "out of town," and her annoying assistant was unwilling to give me any other details other than the fact that my mom was "on vacation."

Right. On vacation without any of the clothes from her hotel? I doubted it.

My next call was to Detective Wanda Knight at the Halo City Police Department. Wanda can be a little bit flaky sometimes—okay, *all* the time—but I trusted that she would take me seriously. I mean, I had pretty much solved her last case for her, so she at least owed me the favor of listening.

When *she* wasn't around, I left a message and decided to wait and see. I waited. And I waited and I waited. Forget the *and see* part.

A week later I was still treading water. There had been no word at all from Isabelle, and the police, unfortunately, had been less than helpful. According to Detective Wanda, if Mom had told someone she was going on vacation, she couldn't be considered a missing person. Being a bad mother and a generally shady individual was apparently not enough to open an investigation.

I was on my own. Déjà vu.

After her initial friendliness Lisa Lincoln had gone MIA as well. I mean, she was around, sort of, but every time I tried to get in touch with her, she was "too busy" to talk, and the return phone calls she had promised never came. I had to wonder why she was avoiding me after she had been so hot to seek me out in the first place. Did she know something that I didn't? Was she hiding something from me?

Ugh. The more I thought about it, the more wound up I got. And the more wound up I got, the more I found that I couldn't make any decisions at all. Of course I was freaking out about my mother, but I really had nothing to go on, and everyone around me kept telling me I was overreacting.

With too many possibilities and no place to really start, the only thing to do was nothing. So I took to my bed.

Not literally, of course. Lying around all week in bed would have bored even *me*. But at the same time, I just couldn't leave the apartment. I couldn't. Daisy called, like, every day, trying to get me to go to the movies or to meet her at Little Edie's or to take a trip to the roller rink and challenge little kids to race us for money. None of it seemed appealing. I thought that Charlie would call eventually, but I didn't hear a word from him.

Not that it mattered. All I wanted to do was hang out on the couch, eat junk food, and read. I was working my way through *Madame Bovary*, which I was enjoying thoroughly. For a couple of days I considered becoming a libertine, but in the end it seemed like too much work, so I gave up on the idea and decided just to become fat instead.

Okay, so I was depressed. I wasn't sure *why*, exactly, but there it was. So sue me.

On the seventh day of my self-imposed exile Theo and my father confronted me. I was basking on the divan by the window, eating peanut butter straight from the jar and wondering exactly what was so great about French linens, when they came marching up. My father stood there with his arms crossed. Theo snatched my precious peanut butter from my grasp and frowned at me.

"Give that back!" I whined. "A growing girl needs protein!"

"Lulu," my father said. "Enough is enough."

"You're depressing us," Theo said. "Every time I walk in here and see you napping on that chaise with the afghan over your face, it makes me want to slit my wrists."

"This was fine for a few days," Dad said. "But you need to get back to your life now. I'm sure that Charlie misses you, for one thing."

"Charlie is trying to prove a point," I said. "Not that it's any of your business."

My dad nodded.

"Charlie hasn't called in a week," I went on, even though he hadn't asked. "He obviously caught on to the fact that I thought he was being too clingy—so he now he's trying to show me how wrong I was by pretending that he doesn't need me at all."

Theo and Dad just kept nodding and smiling at me. I wanted to stop talking, but I couldn't. It was like I was possessed.

"Well, two can play that game," I rambled. "If he's trying to show me who's who by not calling me, then I'm going show him right back by not returning the messages that he's not leaving!"

"I see," Dad said, deadpan. "I'll just keep my nose out of it, then. Anyway, as you know, the Halo Awards are tonight. And as you further know, we are throwing a party, like we do every year. I want to remind you, Lulu, that this is a *regular* party, unlike the pity party that you have been throwing for yourself in your own private universe."

"Please, no," I begged, rolling onto my stomach and burying my face in a pillow. "Not this year! I can't take it!"

I hate the Halo Awards. They're this huge televised excuse for crappy movie stars to get all dressed up, walk down a red carpet, and pat themselves on the back for being so famous. Naturally, they're like a huge holiday for Theo, my father, and their set.

"Lulu, we've been planning this for a month," Dad said. "Now, can we expect you to look respectable for our guests tonight?"

"I always look respectable," I grumbled.

Dad and Theo looked me up and down. Like they had planned it, they each raised one eyebrow in unison.

"What does *that look* mean?" I asked.

"You've been wearing that same T-shirt for at least three days," Theo pointed out. "And it has a tomato soup stain on it."

I examined my shirt. He was right.

"Fine," I said. "I'll change my clothes."

"And condition your hair?" Theo pleaded.

"Okay!" I agreed.

"I want you to invite some friends, too," Dad told me. "No more moping. Isabelle will turn up, I promise. In the meantime, you need to start being sociable again."

"All right, already!" I said. I stood up, let my blanket slide to the floor, and stomped off to my room.

Daisy was the first person to arrive, around seven o'clock. From what I could deduce, her look for the evening was called Fairy

Princess Explodes. She must read different fashion magazines than I do, because last time I checked, Jackson Pollock Meets Cinderella at the Drag Race was not a big trend for summer. Whatever, though; she couldn't *not* look great. As always, she came prancing through the door, teetering on her six-inch heels, with a platter of bean dip balanced carefully on one arm and a layer cake on the other.

"You didn't have to bring food," I said.

"It's from Svenska." Daisy rolled her eyes as if to say, *Can you believe the nerve?* I was excited, though. All other faults aside, Svenska makes a mean bean dip.

"So when does Charles P. Reed show up?" Daisy asked as I led her to the kitchen. "I miss him. I've barely seen him since summer started."

I tried to maintain my usual perky demeanor. "He can't make it," I said. I grinned really huge, like it was no big deal.

"Oh," Daisy said. She put her bean dip and cake on the counter, then turned around and looked at me. "So, are you two still, like, boyfriend and girlfriend?"

"I have no idea!" I said, throwing my arms in the air. "How can he have 'other plans' tonight? What other plans could he have? I know I was a jerk to him, but I'm over it now. And he's still giving me the cold shoulder."

"Hmmm." Daisy tapped her finger to her chin. "Well, I don't know what his deal is, but between the whole thing with your mother and Charlie and whatever, it seems like you could use a party."

"I don't want a party," I said. "I just want to get back to *Madame Bovary*. I'm hoping the end will put me in a better mood."

"I wouldn't count on it," said Daisy ominously.

By the time things were really under way, I was starting to feel slightly better.

Theo had set things up so that the television picture was projected onto a big blank wall at the back of the loft, like a movie screen. When the red-carpet part of the affair began, people began to cluster, crowding onto the couch and squatting on the floor. The pre-show was the important part anyway—all anyone really cared about was making fun of the outfits the celebrities were wearing.

I myself was actually holding out hope that my mother would appear on the screen with some trashy soap-opera stud as her date. Hey; it could happen.

I had a feeling that Dad was thinking the same thing, because as everyone else was talking and joking around, he stayed glued to the projection. His eyes darted intently as he watched, as if he were searching the crowd for a familiar face.

Unfortunately, there was no sign of Isabelle. That would have been way, way too uncomplicated. Instead I was in for a much less pleasant surprise.

About a half hour into the pre-show, Lisa Lincoln came vamping down the carpet. She looked even more gorgeous than usual, with her auburn hair piled onto her head in a volcano of fiery tendrils.

She was poised, elegant, and striking in a delicately stunning emerald green fishtail gown that left very little of her prodigious bosomage to the imagination. Her blue eyes seemed to float a foot in front of her flawless, cherubic face.

A murmur went through the party as she appeared. But it wasn't the way she looked that got their attention. It was her date.

On her arm, dapper and chiseled in a perfectly fitted tuxedo, was Charlie Reed.

My boyfriend.

My mouth dropped open and the room began to swim. Lisa Lincoln had taken *my* boyfriend to the Halo Awards. And I was standing there watching it unfold on TV with practically all of Halo City breathing down my neck.

"Uh-oh," I heard Daisy say softly.

No one else quite knew what to do. I could feel a hundred eyes sneaking glances at me, trying to gauge my reaction. I held my breath. I wasn't going to give them anything. The immortal words of Whitney Houston sprang fortuitously to my mind: *No matter what they take from me, they can't take away my dignity.* I held my head high and smiled.

"Wow. They look amazing!" I said. trying as hard as I could to control the quiver in my voice. "Can you believe that dress? It's gorgeous. I wonder who designed it. It's so cool that Charlie and Lisa have become such good friends!"

I smiled maniacally like this was the best thing that had ever happened to me. *Ever!* The tension in the room deflated, and I gave a small sigh of relief as the collective gaze of the party moved back to the television. Lisa was blabbing to the interviewer, and Charlie was grinning from ear to ear, clutching her tightly around the waist. It was impossible to concentrate on what they were saying.

I have been humiliated many times in my life. Normally I couldn't care less. Or at least I try not to pay too much attention to it. But this was a little worse than any of those times. And by a little I mean a whole, whole, whole lot worse. The room continued to spin.

Thank goodness for Daisy.

"Hey, Lulu," she announced loudly so that the whole room could hear. "My bra is totally too tight. I feel like my boobs are about to get gangrene or something! Could you lend me one of yours?"

Now, this was an absurd proposition for about a million reasons, not the least of which was the fact that Daisy's breasts are about three times the size of mine and there was no way my modest A cups would ever be able to tame her wild chest beasts. I had to smile, just a little bit, though, at her willingness to make a fool out of herself in order to rescue me from a terrible situation.

"Sure, Daisy; I think I have one that will work," I said, and she led me quickly to my bedroom.

"I'm going to *kill* him," Daisy fumed as she shut the door. "What the hell was that?"

I just shook my head. I didn't really have any words. She gave me a hug.

"Oh, Lulu," she said. "It's so utterly obvious what is going on. He's just trying to make you jealous, like a big baby. He's so into you, believe me. I finally blocked him from my buddy list last Tuesday because he wouldn't stop sending me instant messages asking how you were, et cetera."

I flopped onto my bed. "As if I wasn't having a bad enough week as it was." I sighed.

Daisy sat down next to me. "Are you going to be okay? Do we need to stage a prison break to get away from all these people? Maybe we could tie some clothes together and sneak out the window. Let's go to Little Edie's and carbo-load!"

"We're on the seventh floor," I pointed out.

"You have a lot of clothes," she countered.

"No, I'll be fine," I said. I was trying to sound confident, but I was more upset than I was letting on. Yes, Charlie had been coming on too strong. And yes, I had needed my space. But I was supposed to be the one in control of the situation. Charlie was supposed to be madly in love with me.

He wasn't supposed to take no for an answer. And he certainly, *certainly* wasn't supposed to go off and find himself a new, prettier, richer, more *movie star* girlfriend. He was supposed to be sitting alone in his room, listening to Belle & Sebastian and pining. *Pining!*

"What did I do to deserve this?" I moaned.

"Well, you haven't exactly been the best girlfriend," Daisy said. "I don't think anyone is going to dispute me on that tip. But that's no excuse for Charlie to embarrass you. I can't believe him. This is so not awesome. He's going to be hearing from me."

I placed a hand on her arm. "Don't. I let things go too far because

I was afraid to address the problem in the first place. I need to take care of things myself."

"If you say so," Daisy said. "But I still think he's being a little creep." She opened the door a crack and peeked out. "Do you think you're ready to face the party again?"

I took a deep breath.

"I'm ready," I said. If only I'd really meant it.

"Well, let's go, then." Daisy led the way back out into the thick of things.

"I can't even remember the last time my breasts felt this free!" she announced to the room in general, jiggling feverishly. Theo took one look at her and laughed so hard that he had to sit down.

For a while I managed to put Charlie and Lisa out of my mind. My friends really came through, too. Helena Handcart was working extra hard to entertain me, and Alfy Romero flirted with me gamely—just to cheer me up, I'm sure. Little did I know that the Charlie-Lisa surprise had just been a warm-up for the true shock of the night.

The sun was long gone, and the mood in the loft had grown more hushed. The real, serious awards had rolled around, and people had actually started to pay attention. I was perched on the arm of the sofa, next to my father, finally feeling relaxed. I myself was actually daydreaming about what it would be like to own a pet monkey when a familiar face appeared on the screen. I sat up straight as the orchestra tooted a fanfare and the announcer's voice boomed.

"And now, presenting the Most Promising Actress award,

welcome three-time Halo winner and screen legend, the beautiful *Fiona Greer*!"

My father chortled. Out onto the stage strutted the redheaded woman I had spied on at the *Hell Circus* set a week before—the woman my mother had stolen her part from.

"Ah, Fiona," Dad said. "Those were the days."

Theo snorted. I glanced over at him. He was scowling. The room had noticed.

"I don't get it," I said. "What's Theo mad about?"

"I dated Fiona before I met your mother," Dad said, smiling wistfully. "She's quite a lady."

Suddenly I remembered the blind item that Daisy and I had read—the one that had started everything. It all made sense. Mom was Icy Inga—that I already knew. Fiona Greer was obviously Red Rita.

"She's still got her figure," Dad said as Fiona stood at the podium, waiting for the audience to calm down. "Let me tell you, she and I had quite a time. She's a little crazy, but those are always the ones I fall for. You should have seen her back then—legs up to her boobs, and that hair. They used to call her Fiona the—"

"Um, actually? Let's watch the program," I said, cutting Dad off.

Theo shot me a *thank-you* smile. He hates Dad talking about his former flames even more than I do.

My dad quieted down and Fiona, smiling in that smug way of all award presenters, launched into her canned little spiel. "In an industry where the most important words are *beauty*, *Botox*, and *boobies*"—she paused for a moment while the audience, er, *tittered*—"there is almost never a mention of my most favorite *b* word: *brains*. It is therefore a rare and wonderful moment when a young, intelligent actress is able to make herself stand out from the crowd. The women I present to you tonight have all done just that. Yes, they are beautiful, and yes, they are all young enough to be my . . . younger sisters [more canned laughter], but they are one thing above all else: thespians."

Yeah, right. Where I come from, *thespians* wear black velvet capes and hang out by the school auditorium debating whether an Elf could beat an Orc in unarmed, hand-to-hand combat. I had a feeling that Michelle Wigglesworth, the president of the Orchard Academy Dramatic Society, was not up for the Most Promising Actress award. I was right.

"It is with great pride for the *slightly* younger generation that I announce the nominees," Fiona said. She paused for dramatic effect before reading off the names. "Freckle Martinez, for the role of Betsy in *Red, White, and You Know Who!* . . . Dutchie Bouvier for the role of Chastity in *Jack Canfield, MD's, Chicken Soup for the Soul: The Movie* . . ." The camera was panning around the audience, alighting on each contender. Fiona continued, her voice growing more and more portentous with every passing syllable: "Magentta Gundermann for the role of Jodie in *Stephanie Says: The Jodie Sweetin Story* . . . And finally . . ." She looked up and smiled—revealing, I thought, a certain favoritism.

God, it couldn't be.

But it was.

"Lisa Lincoln, for the role of Mary 'Legs' Magdalene in *Teen Jesus.*"

My stomach dropped. Why did I have a feeling I knew which way this was heading?

The audience applauded. I considered hiding my face. This could not be happening.

"And the Halo goes to . . ."

There was a drumroll. Fiona opened the envelope, unfolded it, and let a huge grin spread across her face.

"Lisa Lincoln, for *Teen Jesus!*"

On the screen the audience stood up and applauded. The revelers at my father's party, however, seemed confused as how to react. I clapped, slowly. What else was I supposed to do? After a beat everyone else joined in.

Lisa, for her part, was hopping around on the screen like a Muppet on a caffeine drip. She was squealing and kissing everyone in sight—including, to my chagrin, Charlie—and clasping her chest and squealing some more. Finally, when she was through with the first round of histrionics, she went flying to the stage, where she grabbed her statuette from Fiona and prepared to speechify.

Before she could even begin to address her adoring public, however, a dark look crossed Lisa's face. She opened her mouth, then closed it, then opened it and closed it again. A murmur built in the audience, with Lisa just standing there, flummoxed. Something was going on. The most frustrating part was that we couldn't tell what it was. The camera remained firmly pinned on Lisa: no panning; no cutting away. In my living room we were all mesmerized, trying to divine the origin of the chaos from Lisa Lincoln's morphing expression.

It was probably only like three seconds, but it seemed more like forever. Then, from the side of the frame, they appeared: four tall, busty blond women in hot pink jumpsuits and matching domino masks came storming onto the stage. One of them was swinging a golden lariat; the other three were tossing glitter and flower petals into the audience.

Um. *What?* Was this part of the show? From the expression on Lisa Lincoln's face, I didn't see how it could be.

The woman with the lariat swung it over her head. It flew through the air and, as if by magic, wrapped itself around Lisa's torso. Lisa squealed and wriggled, but the woman pulled the noose tighter. Lisa was trapped.

Lisa screamed at the top of her lungs, and, a minute too late, a team of security guards raced out. The women were prepared. The three ladies on the sidelines handily whipped cans of mace from out of nowhere and dispatched the guards before breaking dramatically into karate poses.

The woman with the lariat approached Lisa and wrenched the statuette from her clenched hand. Lisa gasped indignantly. The blonde stepped up to the podium.

"Ladies and gentlemen," she announced. Her voice sounded familiar. "Ladies and gentlemen, my companions and I are here to tell you that as older women in Hollywood, we will *no longer* be disrespected. We will no longer be cast aside. We will no longer be satisfied playing sassy, no-nonsense judges in courtroom dramas or harridan mothers-in-law in turgid Ben Stiller comedies. In the name of women over thirty everywhere, we claim this trophy for ourselves!" She thrust the golden statue into the air.

Oh my God. I had it now. That voice . . .

My palm flew to my lips and my father grabbed my leg. He had figured it out too, and she was still talking. "We are everywhere. We are your mothers, your sisters, and the women whose posters graced your wall when you were twelve years old. Fear us!"

She ripped off her mask, and my worst fears were confirmed.

"Beware *the Fox*," Isabelle Dark said. There was a pop and a sizzle, and the screen went black.

SEVEN I OPENED THE DOOR THE

next morning to find a penitent Charlie holding a bouquet of flowers. He was looking rumpled and sexy, in a pair of old blue jeans and a worn white T-shirt.

"I don't have time," I said, about to slam the door.

"Sorry, Lulu," he said, thrusting the flowers through the door. "That was crappy of me."

I let him in but didn't accept his peace offering.

"Daisy called you, didn't she?" I asked, tapping my foot pointedly.

"No," said Charlie.

"Is today opposite day?" I asked.

"No," he said. He gave me a sheepish smile.

"If it's opposite day, no means yes," I said.

"I know," Charlie said.

"So she did. Call you."

"Yes. I mean, no," Charlie said. He sighed. "Opposite day is too confusing! Daisy did—I mean, didn't—call me. But I'm still sorry. I didn't mean to embarrass you. And I don't mean either of those things in an opposite way."

I stared at him.

"I made you a mix tape," he said. He dug into his pocket and pulled out a CD, along with a crumpled playlist. My heart melted a little bit, but I tried not to show it. I looked down at the list. The Killers. Check. Death Cab for Cutie. Check. Rilo Kiley. Yo La Tengo. The Mountain Goats. Check, check, check.

"You've been watching too much *O.C.*," I said. "But thank you."

"You're welcome," said Charlie. "Now get over here." He grabbed me and tried to kiss me.

"You must be kidding me!" I exclaimed, pushing him away.

"What?" Charlie asked.

"Saying you're sorry doesn't explain why you were on a televised date with another girl last night. Did you think I wasn't going to find out?"

"Lisa and I are just friends," Charlie insisted. "She's cool and nice. She was supposed to go with Christopher Cardozo, but he canceled at the last minute. She was in a pinch. I was just helping her out."

Lisa had been linked to Cardozo, the star of TV's *Lawson's Pond,* in the past. I supposed Charlie's story had a tiny grain of merit. "What about the fact that you've barely spoken to me in over a week?" I asked.

"I thought you were sick of me. I was just trying to give you space."

"Well . . ." I crossed my arms over my chest.

"Now can we make out?" Charlie asked.

"No!" I said. "And if you thought that making me jealous was a good way to fix things between us, you are so seriously off the mark. Who told you that was a good idea?"

"No one told me anything," said Charlie. "I'm capable of making my own decisions, you know."

"Clearly not good ones," I said, pulling my arms even tighter to discourage him from trying to maul me again. "Listen, Charlie, I'm just not in the mood. In case you didn't notice last night, things are a little bit crazy right now."

"I know they are!" he yelped, his voice breaking. "That's why I brought you flowers!" He thrust the bouquet toward me pathetically, a look of desperation on his face.

But no, I had to be firm in my resolve. I wouldn't be bought off that easily. I don't even *like* flowers. Even though they did look extremely expensive.

"Charlie," I said. "I'm sorry. This is not working out."

"Lulu," said Charlie.

"Charles," I said.

"What are you talking about?" he asked. He looked like he was about to cry. He had dropped the flowers to his side, where they hung sadly. And the worst thing, which I'm sincerely ashamed to admit, is that a part of me *liked* it. I mean, I wasn't happy that I was making him upset . . . but I was back in charge. And that was exactly where I liked to be.

"I think I need some time to think things over," I told him.

"What do you mean?"

"I am an independent woman."

"Thanks for the news flash, Betty Friedan."

"That's not funny," I said. Even though it *was* slightly funny. Only slightly.

"I wasn't making a joke." He sighed in frustration. "I just don't get what your deal is. One minute you're totally into me and the next minute you're saying things like, 'I need some time to think things over.' And you say *I* watch too much *O.C.*? That's like such a WB thing to say."

I walked to the kitchen to boil some water.

"Look," I said. "My life is kind of messed up at the moment. Sue me if I don't really know if I want a boyfriend right now. I have other things to worry about."

"You don't want a boyfriend right now?"

"I'm not sure." I was facing away from him, fiddling with the gas on the stove. I was being rash, I knew, but sometimes that's the only way to be.

"Fine," Charlie said. "I'm not trying to force you into anything here. I want to be where I'm wanted. Get it together, then call me." He dumped the flowers on the counter without ceremony and headed for the door.

Just as he was about to leave, he stopped and called over his shoulder: "I'm sorry about your mother. I hope you figure out what's going on."

"Thanks," I said. Then he was gone.

What had I just done? Had I broken up with Charlie? I wasn't sure. All I knew was that whatever had happened, there was no taking it back.

I finished brewing the tea and sat on the couch, mug in hand, with my legs tucked up against my chest. What was wrong with me? Charlie and I had been friends forever—and things as boyfriend and girlfriend weren't *that* bad, were they? Was it really right for me to cut and run at the first sign of trouble?

A terrible thought occurred to me: Maybe I was more like my mother than I realized.

Just a year ago things had been so different. It was ironic, really. My relationship with Charlie had been more romantic *then*, before we were actually supposed to be boyfriend and girlfriend at all.

Like, last summer Charlie and I took the ferry out to Egg Island, where the really good beaches are—I mean, like, the real beach, as opposed to the beach that's practically in the city. Daisy was on a three-week hiking trip through Pennsylvania with Svenska, so it was just the two of us—me and him. And it was a perfect day weather-wise, with a sky that made you just want to take off your shirt and jump into the waves.

The shore on the island was all umbrellas and trashy paperbacks and pasty bellies that hadn't seen sun in several months. Charlie and I were no exception. We were both whiter than Engelbert Humperdinck, but we didn't care.

He had packed a picnic lunch for us. He'd made it himself. And yes, it was very sweet of him to try. Unfortunately, it was also disgusting. I mean, I don't think Charlie had ever even made himself a PB and J before, much less prepared a gourmet picnic. Basically he seemed to think that *gourmet* translated from French to mean "lots and lots of mayonnaise." He might as well have brought a jar of Hellmann's and some white bread for dipping.

I'd tried my hardest to eat it, but, I mean, after about three bites of my sandwich, I gave up. I had to. Everything was just too . . . globular.

"Charlie, you are a great cook," I said.

"Thanks," he replied, gulping to get down a big, gooey, sun-soggy bite.

"But I think the whole picnic thing just isn't working for me."

He looked wounded for a minute, but then he considered his sandwich. A look of nausea crossed his face. "I guess you're right. It's a little rich, isn't it?"

I searched for the most tactful way to put it. "I think it's just . . . more indoor fare."

"Okay," Charlie said. "Plan B."

I volunteered to go in search of hot dogs and soda—for both of us. I wandered up to the boardwalk, not really paying much attention to where I was headed or, for that matter, where I was coming from.

I guess what I'm trying to say is that I lost him. By the time I'd fetched our food, I had no idea in the world where I'd left my friend. I wandered around for what seemed like forever, searching, scouring the horizon for a sign of him.

But it was no good. I'd become completely disoriented. I didn't even know if I was going in the right direction. I could feel myself getting a sunburn. I had a feeling that I'd traveled miles from where I'd started. My cell phone was in my purse, next to Charlie, and I'd spent my last penny on the hot dogs.

So I sat down on the sand, with absolutely no idea what I was going to do. I hated to admit it, but tears of frustration began to sting at the corners of my eyes. The hot dogs shriveled and turned cold. I was hopeless.

Then in the distance I heard a familiar voice, shouting over the whir of a motor.

"There she is!"

I stood up to shield my eyes from the sun, and there he was, Charlie, riding along on a dune buggy, with a cop at his side.

"I thought something terrible had happened," he said, hopping off the buggy and pulling me into the biggest, most reassuring hug.

He gazed into my eyes. The look on his face was pure relief. "Oh my gosh, Lulu, I'm so glad you're okay."

"It was my fault," I admitted. "I got lost." I grimaced, preparing for the sound ribbing that I, for one, would readily give to any friend who couldn't find her way back from the boardwalk.

But there was no mockery forthcoming.

"Don't worry about it," Charlie said.

I hopped onto the buggy and we rode off, and he never mentioned the incident again—not even to get a laugh out of Daisy.

See, if Charlie hadn't come to my rescue, I'd still be sitting on the beach today. That is, if I'd made it through the winter in my bathing suit. And he was such a gentleman, refusing to share my moment of spazitude with anyone we knew.

If nothing else, I still owed him a hot dog. Right?

I thought about calling Charlie and apologizing. But in the end I decided against it. Once you make a decision, you have to stick with it and not look back. Otherwise people start to think you're some kind of a wimp.

Hmmm, maybe *Charlie* had called *me*. If there was a message on my voice mail begging me to reconsider, maybe I would be able to entertain the notion. I pulled my cell phone out from its customary spot between the couch cushions and checked the messages. There were three. Promising!

Unfortunately, all three of the messages were from the same person, and that person wasn't Charlie. Wanda Knight had been calling me all morning. Since the events of the previous night, the Halo City PD had suddenly become interested in the case of my mother's disappearance. As much as I wasn't feeling the crime-solving spirit, I prepared to head over and talk to them.

The only one way to get your mind off a disaster is to focus it on another disaster, I always say. And this thing with Isabelle definitely qualified as such.

I changed into a pair of black Bermuda-length cutoffs and a secondhand Helmut Lang tube top—my version of business attire—and pulled my hair into a ponytail before walking out the door.

Since the previous day the heat index seemed to have doubled. Moisture hung in the air like a cloud of everyone's excess sweat. This was the part of summer that I couldn't stand, but it was better than winter, I decided. Winter fashions are so not fun.

Wanda greeted me with a maternal hug when I arrived at the station. Her ash blond hair was impeccably tousled, her face was carefully made up, and she reeked pleasantly of Angel, by Thierry Mugler, which kind of smells like how I imagine a houseful of fancy French hookers probably smells. Her *signature scent*, Wanda calls it. "Let's talk, Lu," she said, giving me a quick kiss on the cheek. "Want to take a walk in the park?"

"If you don't mind the heat, I'm game." I nodded. "I think I've already sweated off every drop of moisture in my body."

"Women don't sweat, Lulu," Wanda chided. "We glow."

"Ah," I said, and I followed her out of the building and across the street to the sunny, tree-lined park.

Wanda Knight has this way of being both matronly and glamorous at the same time. It's a neat trick. She's what they call a full-figured gal, but it's all muscle. And she takes care of herself—practically keeps Sephora in business with the volume of cosmetics she must buy. That day, walking through Dagger Park with a no-nonsense stride and the collar of her uniform turned up, she cut quite the imposing figure—even if she didn't have her gun at her hip. She seemed completely unaffected by the heat, which by all rights should have been melting her face right off.

"So, what's going on, Lulu?" Wanda asked.

"I don't know," I told her. "I mean, Isabelle was being spacey, but that's nothing new. I definitely wasn't expecting *this*."

"What's *this*?" she asked. "I mean, what do you think the point of that little show last night was?"

"I have no idea," I said truthfully. "I mean, I really haven't the slightest. What do *you* think?"

Wanda looked me squarely in the eye. "Lulu. I'm going to be straight with you. Your mother is in real trouble. Lisa's people want to press charges against her. Do you want your mom to go to jail?"

My heart beat a little faster at the thought.

Isabelle in jail? She wouldn't survive a day.

"No," I answered.

"Well, listen, then," Wanda told me. "Help us out. If you can find your mom and convince her to cooperate, it would help her case a lot."

I couldn't decide whether to nod or shrug, so I did both.

Wanda was wary. "I know you, Lulu," she said. "You've been nosing around since your mother disappeared. You must have *some* idea of the situation."

"Honestly, I don't. My personal problems have precluded me getting involved," I said curtly.

Wanda raised her eyebrows. "*Personal* problems? Isn't *this* a personal problem?"

"Boy problems," I said. Obviously it was just an excuse. As much consternation as my mother had caused me, I wasn't about to sell her down the river. Not until I did a little more digging.

For now I was going to have to keep certain details to myself. Details such as the article clippings, the impostor maids, the missing photograph—okay, pretty much everything.

I'd gone to the fuzz a week ago about Isabelle's disappearance. They had passed up their chance to get me to talk. I may be a lot of things, but I'm no stool pigeon.

Wanda looked me up and down carefully. "Well, if you think of anything else, give me a call," she said. "You have my celly."

I nodded.

"Want some soft serve?" Wanda asked, stepping up to a street vendor.

"Sure," I said.

When Wanda and I parted ways, I noticed that I had a message on my cell phone. I hastily pressed in the code to retrieve my voice mail. Could it be Charlie?

No such luck. It was from Daisy.

"Lulu," her voice whispered on the recording. "I need you to meet me behind my building ASAP. It's *Svenska*. She's on the warpath. *Beware*. I'll pay you back if you need to take a cab."

I sighed. Another one of Daisy's schemes. Unlike Daisy, I am not enthused by the word *caper*. Why, then, did I seem to attract them? I stepped into the street and raised my arm for a taxi. Anything to stay busy.

I arrived at Daisy's apartment fifteen minutes later and snuck around the building, keeping my eye out for any sign of Svenska. The lot behind Daisy's place looked empty. Just as I was starting to wonder what was going on I heard a creaking noise coming from above my head. I looked up to see Daisy climbing down the rickety fire escape from the seventh floor.

"Thank God you're here!" she called down. "I've been going crazy." She was in her spy gear—a black unitard, with black tights and black ballet slippers. Her hair was slicked back tight, into a severe braid, and she had on a pair of mirrored, wraparound sunglasses.

"What's going on?" I asked.

"Svenska's gone off the deep end. I mean, she really has this time. She caught me drinking orange juice out of the carton and locked me in my room."

Daisy had reached the end of the fire escape. Unfortunately, it was the kind that stopped at the second floor. She peered down at me.

"Now you're stuck." I said.

"Not quite," Daisy replied. And with that she made a running jump and landed perfectly on her feet right in front of me.

"Let's get out oh here. This mystery isn't going to get solved by itself," she said. "And I'm not going to let some little detail like being grounded force me to miss out on the excitement."

"And what exactly is our mystery?" I asked wryly.

"Figuring out where your mother is and what on earth she thinks she's doing terrorizing Lisa Lincoln," Daisy stated.

I didn't say anything. I didn't really know what to say. I was glad that Daisy thought I was capable of tracking down my mother, but I didn't have her confidence.

"I just don't know," I said. "It makes my head hurt to even think about it. The whole thing is too weird, like something out of *Batman*."

"Be serious," said Daisy. "Do you want to rescue Isabelle or not?"

I thought it over. "Yes," I said. "Especially after talking to Detective Wanda this morning."

"Well, lay out the facts, then," Daisy coached. "What do we know?"

I adjusted my glasses in an attempt to feel smarter.

"Isabelle was here to shoot *Hell Circus* with Lisa Lincoln. She took over for Fiona Greer, who was fired at the last minute and wasn't happy about it. Then there was the ransacked trailer . . . and some French maids. And pink jumpsuits and a golden lariat." I paused. "Can you see why this isn't adding up?"

"Well, Isabelle is lost. Like a cell phone. If you lost your cell phone, how would you find it?"

"First I'd look between the couch cushions. That's where it always is."

"Lulu!" Daisy snapped.

"I'd retrace my steps." I shrugged.

"Well, where was the last place you saw her?" Daisy asked.

"Corona Beach," I said.

"Come on, then," said Daisy. "The train fare is on me."

Corona Beach was way different the second time around. That's the thing about carnivals, you know? If you're in a good mood, they're all about cotton candy and funnel cake. But turn your mood only a hair in the other direction and you've got something totally different. You've got roller coasters just one run away from popping a gear. You've got midway barkers who kidnap teenage girls and lock them in a cage in the freak show. This was one of *those* days.

It was the height of the afternoon when we arrived, but the flashing, frantic lights of the midway rides cast the sun in dull contrast. The tinkling, piped-in circus music, running in an endless loop, gave me a headache after about two seconds. And then there were the clowns. Not real clowns, I mean, but pictures of them painted everywhere: crude and garish and grinning. Sinister. I mean, who decided that clowns would be a good idea?

We made our way to the last place I'd seen Isabelle, where her trailer had been parked just over a week ago. We were out of luck. As we walked toward the site of the movie set, it was easy to see that Daisy and I were too late. Where there had once been lights and cables and equipment, there was pretty much nothing. The trailers were gone. There were a few random guys milling around, packing stuff up, but the picture was clear: the shoot had ended.

"Well, so much for that idea," Daisy said. "What now?"

This was a job for my good friend ChapStick. I applied a fresh coat. Unfortunately, it seemed that I had gone to the well one too many times. I wasn't struck by a lightning bolt of inspiration. Not even so much as a little static shock.

"Um, I don't know," I said.

"Let's ask a gypsy!" Daisy suggested, pointing across the midway to a woman in a fortune-telling booth. "Maybe she can use her psychic powers to tell us all!"

I would like to be able to say that I don't believe in psychics or crystals or any of that New Age crap. I really would. But I can tell you from experience that there's at least a little bit of substance to it. Only a few months ago I'd had a very creepy tarot card experience. I wasn't so sure that I wanted to repeat it.

Daisy took my hand and led me, resisting, toward the booth.

"Come on, Lulu," she whined. "Do you want to rescue your mom or not?"

"That's the thing," I said. "I don't really know that my mother needs rescuing. I mean, it kind of seems like she might be some kind of bad guy herself."

Daisy just snorted. "So she dressed up in a costume and pulled a prank," she said. "It doesn't seem so terrible to me."

"Yeah, you *would* think that seemed like a perfectly normal thing to do."

Daisy shrugged. And just then I noticed something out of the corner of my eye. Skulking off in the distance was someone I recognized: it was Fletcher Rose, the director whom I'd seen arguing with Fiona that day on the set. He was wandering around near the haunted house, which had been officially closed years ago due to its terminal unscariness but had never been torn down.

"Look," I whispered to Daisy. "Over there." I pointed to the director.

"A funny little fat man!" she said. "So what?"

"So he's skulking around the haunted house, and it's my opinion that no completely innocent person ever skulks."

"Well, then," Daisy said, "we might as well check him out."

We climbed the creaking wooden steps, trying our best not to make any noise, and crept through the narrow entranceway into the haunted house.

Inside, the house had the dim, abandoned feel of a beach cottage closed for the winter. The mechanical ghosts and skeletons were frozen creepily in place, and there were tiny, dusty rays of sunlight crisscrossing through the cramped, twisting corridors. Somewhere in the distance we could hear the echo of voices. Other people were in there. People besides Fletcher Rose.

I tiptoed toward the sound, with Daisy close at my heels. We made our way through the dark, practically tripping a few times over plastic corpses, trying to ignore the cheesy papier-mâché ghouls. The sound of heated conversation grew louder as I advanced, but I still couldn't make out what was being said.

Then we turned a corner and saw something very bizarre. Ten feet away from us, lit up in a ghostly aura of blue light, was an enormous crowd of people.

"Is a party going on in here?" Daisy asked under her breath.

"Or possibly a genetic-cloning convention?" I asked.

Every one of the fifty or so people that we could see looked exactly the same. Half of them looked just like Fletcher Rose. The other half were identical to . . . Fiona Greer!

It was an eerie sight. To say the least.

"*What* is happening?" Daisy whimpered.

"Shhh," I said. "Let's get closer. Don't make a sound."

It slowly became clear what the deal was: we were approaching a looking-glass maze. Fiona and Fletcher were somewhere in the middle of the maze, arguing with each other, and their images were being multiplied into infinity by the rows and rows of opposing mirrors. Typical of an actress, I thought, to go out of her way to have a conversation in the only place she could gaze at a trillion different images of herself at once.

Fiona and Fletcher were arguing furiously. Daisy and I paused at the threshold of the maze, careful not to let our reflections catch, and listened.

"I was only trying to do the right thing," Fiona said. I could see that she was near tears.

"Yeah, right," he sneered. "You're good at doing that. Doing the right thing."

"Don't accuse me," Fiona sobbed. "After you fired me for that *slattern*. Think about what she did to me! If it weren't for her, things would have been different."

Hmmm. After all these years was it possible that Fiona was still hung up on the fact that my mother had stolen my father from her?

"I told you, my hands were tied," Fletcher argued. "But don't worry. After last night Isabelle Dark is the last person that anyone should be jealous of. She's got problems of her own."

Fiona was about to respond when suddenly there was a sharp, high-pitched trill. Daisy and I both jumped. I realized that I hadn't breathed in at least a minute and a half. Fletcher Rose dug into his pocket and pulled out a cell phone. I exhaled. I guess I was a little bit on edge.

"Yeah?" he barked into his celly. "Oh, *hell* no. Okay. I'll be there ASAP. Tell her to calm down or she'll be sorry. Tell her she has no idea who she's messing with. Got it?"

He flipped his phone shut. "I gotta go," he said to Fiona.

"I hope you know that I love you," Fiona said, wiping her tears.

"I do," Fletcher said.

Fiona leaned in, and it looked for a second like she was going to kiss him.

I cringed in anticipatory disgust. It turned out, however, that my reaction was premature. Instead Fiona just gave Fletcher a big bear hug.

"I love you, Mom," Fletcher said. "And don't worry. Isabelle Dark has no idea what I have in store for her."

Daisy squeezed my leg. Before Fletcher's words could really sink in, though, he began walking straight toward us!

We flattened ourselves against the wall as he approached. The dim corridor we were standing in couldn't have been more than three feet wide.

Oh no! We were about to be discovered!

EIGHT

DAISY WAS CLUTCHING MY hand so hard that I thought it was going to fall off. As Fletcher Rose drew closer, we backed up against the wall as far as we could possibly go—standing on our tiptoes. It was dark enough that it was just barely possible he might miss us—if he didn't trip right over us, that is. And after that threatening phone conversation, this was *not* a guy I wanted to be messing with.

I'm not joking here. I can tell you exactly what Fletcher Rose had for lunch that day: a hot dog with relish and mustard, a Diet Pepsi, and some cotton candy. How do I know this? Because he came so close to us that I could smell it on him. He just squeezed right past, his face only millimeters from mine, never realizing, through some miracle, that he was practically standing on top of two so-called girl detectives who had just been privy to every one of his incredibly suspicious words, not to mention his foul breath.

When the danger of being discovered was past and Fletcher's footsteps were drifting out of earshot, I felt my heart rate slow. Just as the coast seemed clear to sneak out ourselves, I realized that

Fiona Greer was still standing in the hall of mirrors. I turned my attention to her. And surprise, surprise.

"Look, Daisy," I whispered in amusement.

Fiona was mesmerized by the sight of herself in the mirrors, vamping and posing blithely for her own entertainment. Just minutes ago she had been crying, and now she was dancing around like she was on the catwalk. Hands on her hips, tossing her hair, jerking her shoulders back and forth as she swung her hips. With every move she made, an endless array of alternate Fionas—an army of redhead femmes fatales—copied her like a crew of messed-up, over-the-hill Rockettes. And as much as I would like to make fun of her for it, let's face it: there have been times, when I've been alone in my room, when I have been known to work it for the mirror in an extremely similar fashion.

Daisy and I watched for a moment, transfixed by the hypnotic display of synchronization.

"Come on," I finally muttered. "I think we've seen enough."

Back on the midway, Daisy realized that it was getting late. "I've got to get home before my mother figures out I'm gone," she said. She was right. Evening was approaching. Thankfully, that at least meant the heat had subsided a little bit. We walked back to the train.

My mind was swimming with everything that we'd just seen, and Daisy too was uncharacteristically silent. We both retreated into ourselves, privately mulling over the possibilities.

I tried to plot things out in my mind. I've heard that's what detectives do. In fact, I hate to admit it, but since my last brush with intrigue, I had read a few detective novels. Just to see what it was all about. There's one famous fictional, alphabet-oriented lady detective who puts all her stock in writing things down on index cards and shuffling them around in different orders until it all falls magically into place. But that felt a little bit too much like writing a research report for school, plus I didn't happen to have any index cards on my person.

Detective Wanda seemed convinced that Isabelle was the criminal mastermind behind all the strange events that had recently occurred. And though I couldn't say that I exactly disagreed with her, I'm sad to say that I didn't put much stock in my mother to *mastermind* much of anything. I mean, she needs a professional stylist just to mastermind her *outfits*. How was she to be expected to put together, like, a whole elaborate crime operation, even one as absurd as this?

Then there was Fletcher Rose. True, the conversation we had overheard didn't exactly reveal much of anything, but it made him look extremely suspicious.

He had said, "Isabelle Dark has no idea what I have in store for her." What did he mean by that?

Fletcher *was* the one who had replaced Fiona with Isabelle in his little excuse for a movie. Could it be that Isabelle was pulling those pranks on Lisa *according to Fletcher Rose's instructions*? Was Isabelle Fletcher Rose's patsy? That made some sense, I figured.

And Fiona Greer was Fletcher Rose's *mother*? That was an

unexpected development. It was the first I had ever heard of such a thing, and if the tabloids had never mentioned it, it was surely as much of a secret to everyone else as it was to us. Did that give Fletcher a motive for using my mother as a scapegoat? Signs pointed to yes.

"So what's your plan?" Daisy asked as we reached the train station.

"I'm not sure yet," I said. "You're going to head home?"

"Yeah," she said. "If Svenska figures out what I did, you can forget your trusty sidekick until, like, the end of time. She'll lock me up and throw away the key, and even Miss Inez faking a seizure won't be able to get me out of there."

"Okay," I said. "Good luck. I think I'm going to stick around here for a bit until I sort things out. I still don't know what to make of everything we just saw."

"Me neither," Daisy said. "But I don't think I'll ever get the image of a hundred thousand Fiona Greers out of my mind. I'm so traumatized."

"You and me both, Daisy." I sighed. "You and me both."

After she had departed, I wandered over to a concession booth and bought an overpriced cup of Dippin' Dots.

Soft serve and Dippin' Dots. Both in one day. This had to be a low point. But how was I supposed to resist? It was sweltering, and Dippin' Dots *are* the ice cream of the future, you know.

I sat down at a picnic table and pulled out my phone as I ate. I figured I might call Helena just in case she'd picked up some info through secret gossip columnist channels. As I was flipping through my contacts, though, looking for her number, my attention alighted on another name: Jaycee Frost.

Hmmm, I thought. I never had gotten through to my mother's agent.

It was tough to get information out of Jaycee—heck, it was difficult even getting her on the phone—but with a little creativity, I thought I could manage it.

I hit the send button.

"Artistic Creators Agency," a youngish-sounding voice answered. "Jaycee Frost's office."

"I need to speak with Jaycee immediately," I said, with as much authority as I could muster.

"Jaycee's out of the office," the assistant said. "Can I help you?"

It's a good thing that I read pretty much every celebrity magazine, because my longtime devotion had armed me with the knowledge of who, exactly, Jaycee Frost's most important client is.

"This is Natasha Oiseau," I said, raising the pitch of my voice a notch to mimic the notoriously demanding actress. "It's very important that I get in touch with Jaycee *now.*"

The tone of the woman on the other end changed immediately. "Ms. Oiseau!" she exclaimed. "Jaycee's not here, but I'll patch you through to her cell phone right away!" There was a click on the line and I heard it ringing again.

I smiled to myself. Sometimes I'm such a genius.

Jaycee answered her celly after the second ring. "Nats?" she chirped. "What's up? Everything okay?"

"I'm concerned, Jaycee," I said, affecting the actress's inflection to the best of my ability.

"Concerned? What about?"

"Last night. Lisa Lincoln. What's going on here, Jaycee? What if they come after *me* next? Do I need to get another security guard to protect my statuettes?"

"Hmmm," Jaycee said. "Well, I don't know about that, but I've got something else you should be *very* concerned about."

"Oh yeah?" I perked up. Where was she going with this?

"Yeah," Jaycee said. She sounded louder for some reason.

"What is it?" I asked. The suspense was killing me.

"The fact that I'm standing right behind you."

"Wha?" I felt a tap on my shoulder and spun around. Sure enough, I was face-to-face with Jaycee Frost herself.

"Hello, *Lulu*," she said. "Or would you rather that I keep calling you Natasha?"

"Um, hi," I said sheepishly, still clutching my phone to my ear.

"What say we hang up?" she suggested. "No sense in wasting the daytime minutes when we're three inches away from each other."

I just shrugged and dropped my phone into my bag.

"How did you know I was here?" I asked. Jaycee laughed.

"I didn't," she said. "I'm here because I'm looking for your mother. But it seems like they've wrapped the *Hell Circus* shoot."

"Looking for my mother?" I narrowed my eyes at her. "I thought you said my mother was on vacation. So now you're changing your tune?"

"I'm not changing anything," she said. "After last night it's everything else that's changed."

"I see," I said.

Jaycee looked me up and down as if she was trying to decide how much to tell me. The last time I'd been this close to her was when I'd been about ten years old, and she still kind of annoyed me, just like she'd annoyed me as a small child.

It's probably unfair of me, but I've just never liked the looks of her—she's always reminded me a little bit of a rabbit. Her eyes are always darting around, and she has this terrible habit of scrunching her nose up and down while you're talking to her. When I was younger, I'd suspected that she was sending secret messages back to her burrow of evil bunny conspirators. What can I say? I know some people think bunnies are cute, but to me they have a certain sinister quality. Jaycee looks like she is just one step away from descending the evolutionary ladder down to the rabbit warren.

And did I mention the time she stole my carrot sticks? I am not even joking. It was in fourth grade, when I was visiting my mom on the set of *Cheerleader Coven 3*. I was just sitting there, munching on carrot sticks from a plastic baggie, watching them film this scene where mom does this spell that makes the other cheerleaders' skirts fly up, and Jaycee sort of like sidles up to me and just starts making conversation. I don't even know what it was about—nothing, basically—but when I looked up, Jaycee was gone and *so was my little baggie of carrot sticks.* Can you believe this? Candy is one thing, but, I ask you, *What kind of person would steal a child's healthy snack!?*

I asked my mother that question, and she told me that it is exactly the type of thing an agent would do. She said I was lucky that Jaycee didn't snip off my ponytail and sell it to a wigmaker for two dollars.

Isabelle said that agents were supposed to be shifty, and that it was okay, so long as they were shifty on your behalf. By all accounts Jaycee *was* a fierce advocate of my mother's career, so at the very least, I had to give her that.

Jaycee had gotten a lot shorter since I was ten. I mean, I had a good three inches on her now at least.

"Well, you've certainly grown up," Jaycee observed.

"And you've certainly gotten old." I smirked.

"Touché," Jaycee said. She smoothed her ponytail. "Let's talk."

"Fine," I said. "Start talking."

"Not here," she replied. "It's too . . . exposed. Let's go on the Ferris wheel. I don't want anyone to be able to hear us."

The real truth is that I'm slightly terrified of heights—ever since my little roof-climbing adventure a month or so back. But I wasn't about to admit that to Jaycee. "Okay," I told her. "The Ferris wheel it is."

As we waited in the line together, I studied Jaycee as best as I could. Though it had been ages since I'd last seen her, she still looked pretty much the same. She still had the same sleek blond ponytail and the same sleek black outfit that she'd always worn.

Her rabbit face, such as it was, had settled into a certain dignified authority.

"So I hear you're making quite a name for yourself," she told me
as we waited in line together. "Your mother is really proud of you."

"Really?" I asked. "She could have fooled me."

"Well, she is," Jaycee said. "She's always talking about your *mystery*."

"Hmmm," I said, not knowing how else to respond. Why was it that
everyone seemed to know how much my mother adored me but me?

Jaycee turned and looked at me. "Let's hope you can solve this
case, Lulu," she said. "I'm worried. And I'm counting on you."

I didn't say anything, but I was slightly put off by this notion. She
was counting on *me*? Of all people to count on, there had to be
many more sensible choices than me. For one thing, I had just broken up with my first boyfriend! I was *supposed* to be planted firmly
in front of the television with a pint of Chubby Hubby and a box of
Kleenex. But no. People were counting on *me* to solve a mystery, so
here I was.

As annoyed as I was to have this huge responsibility on my shoulders, I would be lying if I said that I wasn't itching to put it all
together. There were so many strange pieces of this puzzle—somehow they all had to fit.

By the time Jaycee and I had made it onto the ride, I was chomp-
ing at the bit to find out what she had to tell me.

"So," I said, when we were under way. "Spill. What do you know
about my mother? What has she gotten herself wrapped up in?"

"You first," Jaycee said. "You've got to have information of your own. If what your mother told me about you is right, then you've surely figured a few things yourself by now."

"Well . . ." I stalled. How much did I want to give away here? I didn't really even know what Jaycee's intentions were.

"I don't know," I finally said. "I haven't really figured out very much."

Jaycee gave me a look of *Cut the crap.* "Lulu, this is not the way we do things in my business. If you want to know what I know, you've got to make a trade. Quid pro quo, or what have you."

We were approaching the top of the ride, and I was gripping the guardrail so tightly that my knuckles had turned completely white. Below us Corona Beach was sinking into a sparkly, candy-colored panorama. As the sun began to set, the neon lights grew brighter and brighter until they defined the landscape at our feet.

"Come on, Lulu." Jaycee leaned closer, causing our car to tilt forward. "This is important, and time is of the essence. Tell me what you know."

I gripped the rails tighter as the car swayed in the summer breeze.

A thought occurred to me. Did Jaycee *know* about my acrophobia? Was that why she had suggested the Ferris wheel? Was she really that desperate to know where my mother was?

If I hadn't been so preoccupied, imagining my own plunging death, I might have made a different decision. But at the time it felt like I didn't have much of a choice. I had to share what I'd learned.

Before I knew it—and against my better judgment—I was giving Jaycee the full scoop in great detail.

"And then," I was saying, "Charlie tried to kiss me. And I was like, 'Oh no, you didn't,' and he was like—"

"Lulu," Jaycee interrupted, her face a mask of impatience. "I'm really sorry about your problems with your BF. You can tell my secretary *all* about it sometime. But could we please get back to your mother? You know, the one who's my *client*?"

I blushed. The stuff with Charlie must have been bothering me more than I'd realized.

"Sorry," I said. Then I thought of something. "Hey, did you know that Fiona Greer is Fletcher Rose's mother?"

Jaycee turned and looked at me quizzically. "No, I'd never heard that," she said. "Where did *you* hear it?"

I finished off the story, relating the scene that Daisy and I had just witnessed a few hours ago in the haunted house, ending with Fiona and Fletcher's strange embrace.

"Wow," Jaycee said when I was done. "That's definitely weird. Fletcher Rose was raised in Pennsylvania. Fiona Greer has been in Hollywood for the last thirty years at least. I don't see how she could be his mother. Are you sure that's what you overheard?"

"Positive," I said.

"Hmmm." Jaycee tapped a long, manicured nail to her lips, as if she was adding it all up.

"Well!" I said. "That's what I know. Now tell me what you know. Who on earth is the Fox? And where did my mother, of all people, learn how to swing a lariat?"

Jaycee laughed. "I can answer the second question pretty easily.

She learned how to use a lasso when she played a cowgirl in *Blame It on the Bandito*. You've seen that one, right?"

"Oh yeah," I said. "I'd practically forgotten she was in that." I almost wished I *had* totally forgotten it. *Blame It on the Bandito* has got to be one of the worst movies of all time. It couldn't even be rescued by my mother's brilliant performance as a sharpshooter with a heart of gold.

"As for your first question, Lulu," Jaycee went on, "that's the trickier one. There have been rumors in LA about someone—or some*thing*—named the Fox for months now. Some people think it's a cult; others think it's a terrorist group. Then there are the people who claim to know for *sure* that it's an organic food commune. All I know is that actresses will disappear for weeks at a time, fall out of contact with everyone they're close with, and then show up back on the scene as if they were never gone in the first place, acting strange and not even able to explain where they've been."

"Acting strange how?" I asked. "It seems like actresses always act insane. How can you even tell the difference?"

Jaycee let out a brassy laugh. "Good point," she said. "I guess when I say *strange* I just mean—I don't know. Kind of spacey. Kind of more out of it than usual. Following weird diets. But I guess you have a point. None of those things are exactly out of the ordinary by LA standards."

"So what do you think my mother has to do with it?" I asked.

"I don't know," said Jaycee. "I was nervous when you called me last week to tell me that she'd disappeared. But I was hoping that it was something else."

"So do you think she's the Fox?" I asked.

"No," said Jaycee. "But you know what? I don't really care. I'll tell you what I care about: the fact that my phone is ringing off the hook. That little stunt your mother pulled last night has completely revitalized her career—which, by the way, needed it. You know what they say about publicity, right?"

"Something like, it's really good?"

"Something like there's no such thing as *bad* publicity," Jaycee said. "Isabelle could have *murdered* Lisa Lincoln and she'd still be as hot as Jessica Simpson on a trip to the center of the gosh-darn earth. No! If she'd murdered someone, she'd be even hotter! Can you even imagine the press she'd get? They'd be blabbing about her in Zimbabwe. How do you say 'pay or play' in Swahili, anyway? They speak Swahili in Zimbabwe, right?"

I shuddered. "Jaycee, I'd really rather not think that my mother would be better off a murdereress."

"Oh, sorry," Jaycee apologized. "It's the agent in me. Seriously, though, you have to have some sympathy for the Fox. Don't you?"

"Are we operating under the assumption that my mother *is* the Fox?" I asked.

"I don't care if the Fox is a marzipan cockatiel," said Jaycee nonsensically. "What I mean is that these people—whoever they are—are right. It's a fact, Lulu. Actresses spend their whole lives working hard, being fabulous, learning their craft, and getting their foreheads shot up with *botulism extract*, and what do we do to them? We make them play second fiddle to a talentless little boob stick like Lisa Lincoln in a horror movie at a *carnival*. Where's the justice in that? I say, if this helps your mother's career, good for her. At least she's making an effort!"

I thought about it for a second.

"So, what you're saying is, you think this is all for publicity?" I asked.

"You better believe it," Jaycee said. "Too bad your mother's not answering her cell phone. If she *was*, I'd tell her that Scott Rudin called, and he wants to know how much back end she wants to play George Clooney's freaking *daughter*. Last week she would have been lucky to get a part as his crippled hag of a parole officer. See what I'm saying?"

"Yes, I see," I said. "What I see is that you people are all completely disgusting. You could give Omarosa Manigault-Stallworth lessons in odiousness."

Jaycee gasped. "Lulu! How did *you* know I represented Omarosa?"

NINE

bright and early, ready to take the world down with a running tackle. Now, I know this probably sounds superficial of me, but I really do think it's important to dress nicely if you want to have a good day. I mean, you should dress to fit your mood. It doesn't always work, but it usually gets you off to a good start.

I looked into my closet and tried to decide how my day would unfold in an ideal universe: a smattering of high adventure in the morning, which would be easily resolved by early afternoon and followed by a delicious gourmet lunch at an outdoor café over which a just-rescued (by me!) Isabelle would acquit herself with flying colors. By the time evening rolled around, Charlie—I bit my lip—yes, Charlie, would take me out for a romantic, whirlwind date, which would stretch far into the night and cover practically every corner of Halo City. It would end in a kiss.

Is that too much to ask for? If it is, it shouldn't be.

Ultimately I decided on a safari-print tennis skirt; green, teal, and khaki-colored tank tops that I layered one on top of the other; a long silver necklace with a shark-tooth pendant; and finally, my pink cowboy boots—for good luck. I let my hair fall naturally to my shoulders, ran my fingers through it a few times, and, after a quick look in the mirror, decided to leave it that way. It was a little wild looking, but sometimes that's okay. It went with my whole jungle princess look.

I put on my glasses and called Daisy.

"Up and at 'em!" I said when she answered. "I hope you're not grounded today, because it's time to go detecting! We have an over-the-hill starlet to track down!"

"Lulu," she grumbled into the telephone. "It's early. I haven't had my morning coffee yet. For your information, I haven't even gotten out of bed. I still have my sleep mask on."

Daisy is notoriously difficult to rouse in the mornings. I was actually kind of shocked that she had even gone so far as to pick up the phone. But now that I had her, I wasn't going to let her get away. If I didn't force her to make a plan, she would just go back to sleep as soon as I hung up.

"Come on!" I said. "No time for lying around. Meet me at the subway in a half hour. We have places to sneak into and people to shake down!"

"Lulu," Daisy said firmly, "I am not doing one stitch of investigating until I have a cup of coffee and a healthy breakfast in my system."

"Can't you just eat a granola bar?" I asked.

"As you know, I am very opposed to teen anorexia," she said. Her voice was still froggy from sleep. "And we're both getting a little spindly if you ask me. Let's go to Little Edie's and put on a few pounds. *Then* we can go a-solvin'."

"Fine!" I said. "I hope we're at least eating for free."

"Naturally," she said.

An hour later we were sitting at a window table at Little Edie's, chowing down on a huge breakfast of pancakes, eggs, and bacon. Daisy had plopped an entire pot of coffee in the middle of our table. Since she waits tables at Little Edie's three nights a week, she gets the run of the place on her days off.

"So," she started in. "Did you figure anything else out after I left the carnival?"

"A little bit," I said. "I ran into Jaycee Frost. It turns out she's been hearing about the Fox for a while. She just doesn't know who it is or what it's all about."

"Hmmm," said Daisy. "So it's got to be Fletcher Rose, right? He's the Fox?"

"No, I don't think so," I said. "Actually, I'm pretty sure that the Fox is my mom and she's doing all of this for publicity."

Daisy chewed on a bite of scrambled eggs. "That makes no sense," she finally said. "At the Halo Awards your mother was talking *about* the Fox. Like, in the third person. If she *was* the Fox, she wouldn't do that, would she?"

"Maybe she was just talking in the abstract or something," I suggested. "You know, for dramatic effect." It's possible I was being stubborn, but sometimes you just have to trust your instincts. "It *is* her," I continued. "It's the only thing that makes sense."

Daisy looked dubious. "It seems to me that we have at least one other suspect worth—"

Just then my handbag began to vibrate. My phone was ringing. I checked the caller ID. It was Helena Handcart.

"What's up?" I answered.

"Lulu!" she exclaimed. "Where are you? I need to talk to you in person. It's urgent."

"Um, I'm at Little Edie's with Daisy. We're having a big breakfast. Is everything okay?"

She didn't answer my question. "I'll be right over," she said breathlessly, then hung up without even saying goodbye.

"What did she want?" Daisy asked when I'd clicked off the phone.

"I don't know!" I said.

"Well, what did she say?"

"Nothing! She just said it was urgent. She's coming over to talk to us in person."

"Ooh," Daisy said. "Suspenseful!"

I frowned into my coffee. "Really. And the last thing I need in my life is more suspense."

"Let's eat some more bacon. Nitrates always calm me down," Daisy suggested. She grabbed the platter and flitted off to the kitchen.

Leave it to a seven-foot-tall drag queen to make a grand entrance. When Helena arrived about fifteen minutes later, it wasn't by foot or by train, or even by taxicab or limousine, but on the back of a brand-new, salmon pink Vespa moped. She skidded to a screeching halt right outside our window and tossed her thick mane of hair over her shoulder. When she caught us staring at her, she pursed her lips, cocked her head saucily, and gave a huge, mascaraed wink, like an eighties music video vixen.

"This better be good," I said.

"It certainly *looks* important," Daisy pointed out. "Helena's not even wearing a full face of makeup. When have you ever seen that before?"

She was right. Helena had obviously left in a hurry. She came storming into Little Edie's still in her pink plaid flannels. Her red curly wig, which had sparkled so spectacularly when she had dismounted her motorcycle, was clearly askew. Most shockingly, as Daisy had noticed, she was wearing only the most minimal (for her) makeup. Something *was* going on. She slid in next to me at the table.

"I came as fast as I could," she panted.

"Well, don't keep us in suspense or anything," I said. "What's happening? Does it have to do with the Fox?"

I was on the edge of my seat, waiting for Helena's news, but in the split second since her entrance she had become distracted by the mountain of food that Daisy had summoned forth. "This looks delish!" Helena declared. "Mind if I have a bite?" She scooped up a huge stack of pancakes without waiting for a response, then went to work on the fixin's. "Is this real maple syrup or imitation?" she asked.

"Could you please tell us what happened?" I prodded. "We're dying here."

"Oh, right—sorry." Helena stuffed her mouth full of food. She was about to shovel in a second bite when I slapped at her hand and glared. She quickly gulped down her pancakes and set her fork on her plate.

"I got a phone call this morning," she said. "And you will never, ever, in one *billion years* guess who it was from."

I had to restrain myself from yelling. Instead I just snapped: "We don't have one *billion years* to sit around trying to guess who called you! So tell us now before we all miss the best part of our lives figuring it out!"

"It's just an expression," Helena huffed. "But anyway, it was your mother."

My jaw dropped. "My mother called *you*? Are you sure? How did you know it was her?"

"Well," Helena said. "I mean, she didn't *say* she was your mother. She didn't identify herself at all. But it *was* your mother. I'd know Isabelle Dark's voice anywhere. I've seen *The Spiteful Heart* at least sixteen times."

"I love that movie too!" Daisy exclaimed. "Especially the part where she hitches the ride from the sheep farmer and winds up at the embassy ball and she's the toast of European society? That is so the best part. But Lulu never wants to—"

"Aaagh!" I wailed. "Could you two *please* stick to the subject? Helena, you were just getting to the good stuff."

"Sorry, little fern," Helena said. She cleared her throat. "So. Anyway. I was woken up at quite an ungodly hour this morning with a supposedly 'anonymous' tip from this 'mystery' lady—who was really Isabelle, as we have unanimously decided. She wanted me to print something in my column. She called it a tip, but it was really an announcement. That's okay, though, because it certainly piqued my interest. She . . ." Helena suddenly paused, searching her memory. "Hold on." She grabbed her oversized purse and dug around inside. "I wrote it down somewhere."

I drummed my fingers on the table until finally Helena retrieved what looked like a crumpled-up face blotter from deep in her handbag and began to meticulously unfold it. She cleared her throat again, preparing to read aloud, and then changed her mind.

"Oh, just read it yourself," she said, and slid it across the table. I snatched it up with a strange mix of eagerness and dread.

Here is what it said, transcribed in Helena's ornate, flowery script:

6/17 – 9:30 a.m.
(Isabelle Dark???)
Announcement from the Fox. Wrinkle Revolution. Actions will continue across Halo City. Meet demands or else! I have chosen to stay and fight.

"I don't understand any of this," I said to Helena. "'Wrinkle Revolution'? What is that supposed to mean?"

"'I have chosen to stay and fight . . .'" Daisy muttered to herself. "That sounds familiar. Didn't someone famous say that once?"

"Oh, she was talking a whole bunch of crazy talk," Helena explained. "I barely understood half of it myself."

I considered things, taking into account my conversation with Jaycee Frost the previous day.

"My mom's agent said that the Fox is some, you know, some

Svengali or something. Like that guy who invented the Backstreet Boys or *NSync."

"Justin Timberlake?" Daisy asked.

"No," I said. "I'm talking about the old man who thought it would be a good idea to get a bunch of teenagers together and make them dance. And boss them around, et cetera. Jaycee says the Fox has all these actresses in her thrall, and she feeds them a bunch of garbage about how they're fighting for the equality of long-in-the-tooth actresses, but really all they're doing is taking orders from her and fetching her coffee. She's the one getting all the publicity out of it. They're just dressing up in funny costumes and causing trouble all over the place."

"The nerve of them!" Daisy said.

That day she was wearing a teal unitard, ultra-short Daisy Dukes, and a pink terry-cloth headband. I didn't pay her any mind.

"What makes you think the Fox is a *she*?" Helena asked.

"I don't," Daisy put in. "I think the Fox is Fletcher Rose! You should have heard him yesterday, Helena. He might as well have had pointy little ears and a fluffy red tail pinned to the back of his pants. Lulu is just being pigheaded."

"I am not being pigheaded," I snapped back. "It's all about publicity. What kind of publicity does Fletcher Rose get out of this?"

"Well," Helena mused, "Your mother *is* in his movie. So any publicity for her is publicity for him."

I folded my arms across my chest. "Don't take Daisy's side!"

"I'm not taking anyone's side!" Helena said. "I'm just thinking things through. It seems to me that you're awfully eager to blame your mother."

"What?" I asked incredulously.

"Sorry," Helena said. "I just mean that you're always a little per-snickety when it comes to your mother."

"Like she hates her guts," Daisy said.

I pouted.

"So maybe you're a little too eager to blame her for every little thing that happens," Helena finished.

In that moment I had to wonder—hadn't Helena and Daisy been in the same room with me when my mother appeared *on national television*, wearing a jumpsuit and swinging a lariat?

What planet were my breakfast mates on, anyway?

"Let's move on," I said. "This message mentions *demands*. What demands is she talking about?"

"Oh, you know these wacky art-terrorist types," Helena said. "They've always got a crazy list of things they want, and none of it ever makes any sense. Enough oatmeal and dried mangoes to feed everyone in China, free rhinoplasty for anyone with a SAG card. Things like that. The Fox—I mean, your mom or Fletcher or whoever—kept talking about 'demands,' but I forgot to ask what the demands actually *were*. I wasn't really paying attention; I was too busy trying to write it all down. It doesn't matter, though. I'm sure they're making it all up as they go along."

"Well, what *actions* do you think they're going to stage?" I asked. "Do you think we should be worried?"

Helena snorted. "No. Not unless your name is Lisa Lincoln."

"Oh, jeez," I said, rubbing my forehead.

"What?" Daisy asked.

"Helena's right. Lisa Lincoln has been the target of all the Fox's attacks. We should really tell her what we know."

"That lying, boyfriend-stealing wench?" Helena asked. "Why do you need to tell her? You don't owe her nothin'."

"I know," I said, "but what if they pull something that's actually dangerous? It would suck if I had the chance to warn her and didn't. That would be just totally petty. Plus if it's my mom behind it all, it's my responsibility to make sure no one gets hurt."

"Why?" Helena screwed up her face.

"Honor," I said. "I have to protect my family honor. I saw it in an old samurai movie once."

"Well, I admire you, Lulu," said Helena. "You're a bigger woman than I."

I tried not to laugh. I knew it wouldn't be sporting of me.

I looked down at our breakfast dishes. We had completely decimated the food and I was feeling hopped up on maple syrup. "Let's get this show on the road," I said. "Next stop, Dagger Hotel. Then we're off to uncover just what my mother is wrapped up in."

I stood up and began busing our plates.

"Lulu, goose, I can't come," Helena said.

"Why not?" I asked.

"Oh, just look at me!" Helena gestured to her face, then her wig, then her pajamas. "I can't go to the Dagger Hotel looking like this. I shouldn't even be out at all. What if my *public* sees me?"

"Helena . . ." I whined.

"How about this," she suggested. "I'll let you borrow my brand-new Vespa to get up there!"

"Ooohhh," Daisy cooed. She loves a fast vehicle.

"You're sure you can't make it, Helena?"

"I'm sure," she said. "Just be careful. Don't get into an accident!"

"I won't," I promised her, and she reached into her pocket and pulled out a set of keys.

"Yay!" Daisy cheered. She grabbed my hand and dragged me outside, where we hopped right onto the bike—me in front and Daisy in back, because she doesn't have her driver's license.

Helena pulled a pink silk handkerchief out of her blouse and began waving it in the wind. "Au revoir!" she said. "I'm getting all misty-eyed! My little girls, saddling up for their first motorbike voyage!"

"Svenska would have an aneurysm if she knew we were doing this!" Daisy whispered into my ear.

"I know!" I said.

I revved the engine, and we were off.

TEN YOU SHOULD REALLY TRY SEEING

Halo City from the back of a brand-new moped sometime. I guarantee it's like nothing you've ever experienced before.

For one thing, it's very blurry—just a messy collage of streaky neon lights and flying billboards. Daisy and I sped through the city, hair streaming behind us, twisting and pivoting through traffic like we owned the streets. Daisy was loving it. So was I. *This* was summer. I could feel it seeping in through my pores.

"We should do this more often!" Daisy shouted as we curled around Bunsen Place, barely avoiding an old lady with a shopping cart full of cantaloupes.

"Hold on!" I replied, pulling a quick hairpin turn down Washington Ave.

I had to agree with Daisy. The feeling was pretty liberating—it almost made me forget my ginormous woes of the past few days. When we pulled up in front of the Dagger Hotel a few minutes later, I totally didn't want to stop.

"Can't we just ride around all day?" Daisy asked. "We can handle the important stuff tomorrow."

"I wish," I said. "But time and tide rest for no girl. Let's go." I swung my leg off the bike and hopped onto the sidewalk, trying to be delicate as I extracted a third-degree wedgie.

"Lisa Lincoln really doesn't deserve this," I grumbled. "But I do feel obligated, and besides, it will give me a chance to ask her more about my mother. She might know something that she forgot to mention the first time around. Or she might have found something out since then."

"True," Daisy said. "I hadn't thought of that."

I smirked at her. "Well, start thinking. If you're going to be my sidekick, you need to learn to stand on your own two feet."

Since I'd been here once before, I knew the way to La Lincoln's hotel room. Daisy and I strode across the polished marble floor of the lobby and took the elevator up to the thirtieth floor. When the elevator doors slid open, we found none other than Trish Archer, Lisa's hulking, ice blond bodyguard, stationed in the corridor.

Trish reminded me of a robot, the way she always had her hair in the exact same tight French braid and always stood in the same exact position, with her hands on her hips and her elbows straight out, her arms forming precise forty-five degree angles. I did admire her makeup technique, though. She always had that natural, summery look.

"Hi, Trish," I said.

She smiled primly. "Hi, Lulu."

"Can we talk to Lisa?" I asked. "It's really important."

"No," Trish said. "She's very upset right now. She doesn't want any visitors—especially you. Your mother stole her statue, remember? There's going to be a lawsuit."

"Well, Lisa stole my boyfriend, so we're even," I countered, trying to walk past her broad, padded shoulders.

Trish put a hand on my arm, stopping me. "That's not the way I heard it," she muttered.

"Me neither," Daisy said under her breath.

I didn't have time to bicker with either one of them.

"Come on, Trish," I whined. "Cut me a break. I really need to see Lisa. I'm doing her a big favor right now."

"You can leave a message," Trish said. "I'll make sure she gets it."

Now, I *could* have left a message, I suppose. But I was annoyed. I had come all this way to do a good deed, and now Lisa was going to pull her diva routine? I'm sorry, but you don't get to start acting like Mariah Carey until you've actually stolen an ice cream cart from a street vendor and wheeled it onto the *TRL* set, throwing cones willy-nilly into the crowd.

"Oh, come on, Trish," I said impatiently, shoving past her to knock on the door. It was a bad move. The next thing I knew, I was on the carpet, lying on my back, seeing stars. Trish had flipped me with some kind of crazy judo move. It turned out this lady wasn't just for show.

Little did she know that I travel with a formidable one-woman security force of my own.

Needless to say, on seeing me attacked, Daisy sprang into action. All I could do was lie there, stunned, as the showdown took place.

Daisy wound herself up slowly, first striking her infamous praying mantis pose: she lifted one knee to her chest and raised both arms straight above her head, fingers curled forward into little claws, as she uttered a nasal, high-pitched battle cry.

"Eeeiayeee!" Daisy squealed.

Trish Archer looked like she was about to burst out laughing. I felt sorry for Trish. Yes, Daisy looked ridiculous. But this was just the prelude. In a second, Trish wasn't going to know what hit her.

Suddenly there was a flurry of arms and legs as Daisy spun, cyclone-like, through the air toward the Amazon. *"Aaaieee!!!!"* she screamed. Have I mentioned yet that Daisy is very, very good at the obscure but deadly art of Icelandic kickboxing?

Thump. Daisy connected handily with a loud blow to the solar plexus. Her burly opponent, caught off guard, bounced up against the wall of the corridor, a shocked expression plastered across her face.

Clearly she wasn't used to being messed with.

Unfortunately, her surprise didn't last long. It was only a split second before Trish collected herself and rebounded with a swift roundhouse kick that just barely missed Daisy's jaw.

"Yaaaiahhh!!" Daisy shrieked. She sprang back several feet only to launch herself into the air for her trademark flying unicorn move. *"EeeeeEEE!"* she cried, tackling Trish to the ground.

Just then the door to Lisa Lincoln's hotel room opened. We all froze. And who do you think was behind it?

No, it wasn't Lisa Lincoln.

No, it wasn't my mother.

No, it wasn't Princess Diana, resurrected from the grave and stealing from the minibar.

It was one Charles P. Reed.

"Trish? Daisy? Lulu?" He looked back and forth in utter befuddlement between the three of us. I took the opportunity to pick myself up off the ground and brush myself off, trying to maintain as much dignity as was practical. Daisy and Trish looked up from their entanglement.

"Uh, hi," Daisy said.

"Is there some kind of fight going on out here?" Charlie asked.

"N-no," I covered. "We just . . . came to see Lisa, and Trish . . . had a spider crawling across her shirt. We were trying to smush it when things started to get out of hand."

Charlie looked at me, all skepticism. I didn't bother saying anything else; it wasn't worth it. I just pushed past him into the hotel room.

And oh, what a sight it was inside. There, in her bed, with the lights dimmed, was the famous Lisa Lincoln, wan and puffy-faced, with a cold compress on her forehead, used tissues strewn in a mountain around her. On the television *Center Stage* was playing with the volume muffled. Lisa was sniffling. She was wearing an outlandishly oversized pair of Gucci sunglasses and sipping from a two-liter bottle of Evian through a straw.

Oh, *please*. Just because of the awards debacle? How pathetic!

I made up my mind then and there. If any daughter of mine ever tried to become an actress, I'd totally disown her. They are all just way too *dramatic*.

Time for a little tough love. I marched over to the television and turned it off. Lisa sat up with a start. "Lulu Dark!?" she exclaimed. "What are you doing here? I'm watching *Center Stage*!" She looked around frantically. "Trish? How did she get in here!?"

Trish, Charlie, and Daisy all stepped into the room.

"I tried to stop her," Trish said. "But *Charlie* let her in anyway."

Lisa collapsed onto the bed again. "Ugh," she moaned, resigned.

"Do you want me to show them to the lobby?" Trish asked.

"It's so not worth it," Lisa whined. "What do you want, Lulu? And make it quick. I'm not feeling so hot since your mother and her ter-rorist friends victimized me in front of the whole entire world and made me the laughingstock of Halo City!"

"Don't blame me," I said. "I *told* you Isabelle was a total crackpot. Plus I'm here to warn you about something."

Lisa rolled over but didn't sit up. "Warn me? About what? How could it get any worse than *this*?"

I rolled my eyes. "I can think of a bunch of different ways, actually."

"You could have the croup," Daisy jumped in. "That always seemed like it would suck. Or you could have amnesia or—"

"Daisy," Charlie interrupted. "Enough already."

"Traitor!" she muttered at him with a sidelong glance.

I turned my attention back to Lisa and related what we had learned from Helena that morning. She looked panicked.

"You think they're going to come after me again?" she wheezed, still sprawled on her side. "Charlie, I can't take it!"

Lisa craned her neck around, looking for her newfound care-taker. He made a move toward her. I gave him my death stare, and he stepped back again, looking entirely unsure of himself.

"Listen," I said. "It's going to be fine. I just wanted to let you know ahead of time, before it's published in Helena Hears. You need to be careful. And I just want to ask you one more thing: Is there anything you didn't tell me before? Does Isabelle have any reason to be coming after you?"

Lisa sat up, flipped her sunglasses over her head, and took a long sip from her water. "Well . . ." she mumbled. "I wasn't going to say anything, but . . ."

"But what?" I asked.

Lisa toyed with her hair. "We kind of got into a fight the night before she left."

"A fight? Why didn't you tell me?"

"It didn't seem like a big deal," Lisa said. "Plus I don't know, your mother was always so worried about what you thought of her. I was just trying to be loyal. I didn't want to talk trash about her."

Isabelle cared what I thought about her? Now, that was ironic. If Isabelle wanted me to think more highly of her, she could have just, you know, been around. And not become a terrorist.

"Well, forget that," I said to Lisa. "What was the fight about?"

"It wasn't really a fight," she said. "More like an argument. She was pissed off at me."

"Why?"

"She found out that I'd helped her get the part in *Hell Circus*. I mean, she was the best person for it for sure, but . . . I kind of asked the producers to replace Fiona with Isabelle. Fletcher was against it, but I'm a lot more important than he is—I mean, no fourteen-year-old in her right mind is going to care who directed *Hell Circus*, but they'll care that I'm in it, and that's all that matters. I thought I was doing Is a favor—she really needed the work. But when she found out about it, oh, man. She was so mad. She had this whole thing like about how she wanted to earn the part on her own. But who earns *anything* in Hollywood? It's *always* about who your friends are. And your mother is—I mean, *was*—friends with me. Me being the most promising newcomer. She should have just gone with it. I don't know how I deserved *this*."

"I don't either," I said, and in that moment I was torn. Yes, Lisa Lincoln had messed with my boyfriend. Yes, she had been a total flake. And yes, she was lying in her hotel bed drinking Evian and wearing Gucci sunglasses in the dark. Still, I felt like I had a responsibility to clear up this mess. It sounded like my mother had betrayed her big-time. I wish I'd been surprised.

"There's something going on here that I don't get," I told her, "but I'm going to figure it out."

We all stood there looking at each other. I caught sight of Charlie and suddenly remembered that he was there but that he hadn't arrived with me. I became instantly uncomfortable. I stared at him. He stared at me. Daisy and Lisa stared at both of us. Trish still looked ready for a fight.

"Well," I said.

"Well," Charlie repeated.

"Sorry, guys," Lisa cut in, "but I'm still feeling really worn out, and I was just getting to the most exciting part of *Center Stage*. I'm going to have to ask you to leave."

"Uh, sure, okay," I stammered. Charlie, Daisy, and I turned to walk out.

"Charlie, I didn't mean *you!*" she called as we were heading out the door. "Why don't you get me a Toblerone from the minibar and watch the rest of the movie with me?"

I cocked an eyebrow at Charlie and scowled. His face blanched in abject fear as he looked back and forth between me and Lisa Lincoln. She drummed her nails on the nightstand. He was no match for her.

Sorry, he mouthed in my direction. He headed straight for the chocolate stash. What a wimp.

Without another word, Daisy and I left the room and headed downstairs to the lobby. What else was I supposed to say? There was really just no point on even commenting. It was all so out of hand.

I couldn't believe Charlie. I mean, *I couldn't believe him.* I know it was the worst time for me to be thinking about my love life, but seriously! How could he be so disloyal? I needed him! At a time like this, he should have been supporting me—not feeding Lisa Lincoln chocolate from the minibar.

Okay, maybe I had asked for it. But he had asked for me to ask for it. Hadn't he?

Ugh. How had we gotten ourselves into this?

Remind me in the future never to get in another relationship. If this is what relationships are like, I will happily drift into old age as a spinster. It's just not worth it.

Daisy and I were gearing up to jump back on the bike when my phone rang again, the screen displaying a strange number that I didn't recognize.

"Hello?" I answered. "Who is this?"

The line was staticky, but I could just make out a familiar, hysterical voice on the other end. "Lulu! I—they're going to kidnap her!"

There was the sound of a scuffle. I heard a horn beep and instinctively pulled the phone from my ear. Then the line went dead.

I heard the horn beep again.

Wait a minute. I looked at my phone. Why was that horn still beeping when I'd lost my connection?

Before I had time to ponder the question, all hell broke loose around us, right there on the sidewalk in front of the Dagger Hotel.

Out of nowhere a throng of suit-clad security guards came racing out the door, walkie-talkies buzzing at top volume. They shoved past us, practically knocking me over, and raced right out into the street.

"Where'd they go? What are they driving?" one of the guards shouted.

"What's going on?" I asked, to no response. The guards were too busy blocking traffic and screaming at each other to pay any attention.

"They must have left through the back!" someone yelled. "Cut them off at the corner!"

"What is going on?!" I shouted.

Just then Trish Archer came staggering out the door. Her hair was shockingly askew, and she had a tear in her collar. The guards were on her.

"What did you see? How many were there? Which exit did they take?" they asked all at once.

"What is going on???!!!" I screamed at the top of my lungs.

Everyone turned and looked at me.

"Charlie and Lisa have been kidnapped," Trish said. She went straight back to her frantic conversation with the security guards.

And then I heard that same horn beeping again—the one I'd heard on the phone with my mother. It all came together—my mother had been calling from the getaway car.

Beeep! There it was again. And it was coming closer.

"Daisy!" I panted. "Quick, hop on!" We slid onto the Vespa. I revved the engine.

At that instant, while everyone was focused on Trish, a huge black SUV came skidding around the corner, speeding like nobody's business, horn blaring, as all the other traffic cleared the street to make way.

Bingo! It was one of those moments that seems to go in slow motion. It was do or die.

"Ready to be an action hero?" I asked Daisy. There was no need to wait for an answer. I gunned the throttle and took off after the SUV.

ELEVEN I WANT TO REMIND YOU,

readers, that high-speed motorbike chases are not safe, glamorous, or in any other way okay, especially if, like me, you don't really know how to drive a motorbike or even really a regular bike, for that matter.

They are, however, still very fun. All that adrenaline pumping, the wind in your face, your hair whipping around in every direction, and a black SUV barreling down the road about to get away with your sometime boyfriend, who will surely forgive you for your many transgressions if you can only rescue him from certain doom.

But let's forget the boyfriend business for now; can we? Whatever the various mysteries of our romantic status happened to be, Charlie was one of my top two best friends on earth, and the other one was clutching at my waist, hanging on for dear life as we sped down the blacktop in pursuit. I couldn't let him get away. If anything terrible happened to him, I'd never forgive myself.

Two blocks in the distance I could see the getaway car speeding across Sycamore Street, and I hunched over on the handlebars and revved the engine. If we could just gain a little ground, we might be able to catch up with them at a light or something. Did kidnappers stop at traffic lights?

"Faster!" Daisy egged me on. She slapped my thigh like I was a racehorse.

The right lane of traffic was completely clear, so I made for open pavement. *"Hold on!"* I warned Daisy, and twisted the handle of the bike as far as it would go.

"Yay!" Daisy squealed. We bumped onto the sidewalk. Pedestrian traffic came to a standstill as we whizzed by. I could hear the faint whine of sirens in the distance.

Yes! We were gaining on the SUV, the gargantuan size of which seemed to be hampering its ability to maneuver through traffic. By the time it turned off onto Tyler Place, by the park, we were a less than a block behind it. Feeling like a total pro, I made the hairpin turn with ease, sticking my leg out a little for balance.

"YAY!" Daisy whooped. "FASTER!"

"I CAN'T GO ANY FASTER!" I yelled above the roar of the engine.

"WHAT WAS THAT PHONE CALL YOU GOT ANYWAY?!" she screamed.

"IT WAS MY MOTHER!" I replied, my voice starting to get hoarse. "SHE WAS WARNING ME ABOUT THE KIDNAPPING!"

"WARNING YOU?! IF SHE'S THE FOX, WHY WOULD SHE DO THAT?!"

"DAISY, I HAVE TO WATCH THE ROAD!" I screeched. "OR WE'RE GOING TO LOSE THEM!"

"YOU'RE DOING FINE! I JUST DON'T UNDERSTAND WHY YOUR MOTHER WOULD WARN YOU THAT SHE WAS ABOUT TO KIDNAP LISA AND CHARLIE!"

"DON'T YOU EVER WATCH TELEVISION?" I shouted. "CRIMINALS LOVE TO

GIVE ADVANCE WARNING! IT MAKES THEM FEEL SNEAKY AND IMPORTANT!"

"LULU, I THINK YOU NEED TO THINK THIS THEORY OVER A LITTLE BIT MORE!"

"OKAY!" I screamed back. "I PROMISE I WILL THINK ABOUT IT LATER. BUT RIGHT NOW WE ARE IN THE MIDDLE OF A HIGH-SPEED—"

Just then I saw an old man step out of the doorway of an apartment building. He was puttering along with his walker, crossing in front of us.

"CRAP!" I screamed, honking the horn and swerving. The man looked up, unconcerned, and waved feebly.

Daisy screamed at the top of her lungs, a high-pitched banshee wail, as we went flying over the curb and through an intersection, barely missing a woman walking her dogs.

We hit the sidewalk on the opposite side of the street, flew upward in an Evel Knievel–style arc, and landed together in a tangle in Dagger Park.

"Ouch," I croaked.

"Are we dead?" Daisy mumbled. "Is this heaven?"

I sat up slowly. "I don't think so. If this were heaven, Jake Gyllenhaal would be here, feeding us strawberries."

Daisy sat up. She seemed fine. A quizzical look spread across her face as she turned and looked at me appraisingly. "Do you even *know* how to ride a Vespa, Lulu?"

"You *would* blame me for this," I moaned. We both collapsed again onto our backs. The sirens that I had heard on the bike grew louder and louder.

A minute later Detective Wanda Knight was standing over us, looking disapproving.

"Hello, Lulu," she said.

I looked up from my repose.

"It was Daisy's fault," I said weakly.

Then everything faded to black.

How's that for a girl-detective-worthy cliffhanger?

I woke up from my little nap and discovered that everything had gone totally, *totally* insane.

Lisa Lincoln, as we all know, is a movie star. But Charlie Reed is incredibly rich. Filthy, stinking rich. His dad is a successful lawyer or something like that, but the main reason he's rich is because, like, two hundred years ago, his grandfather, Aloitius Reed, founded this company that manufactured shoelaces.

You wouldn't think that shoelace manufacturing would make you the sort of money that your great-great-grandchildren would still be living off of, but you'd be wrong. Apparently the shoelace biz is incredibly lucrative.

And here's the thing. When a regular person gets kidnapped, it's bad news. It probably makes Channel Six in the Mix! News at Eleven. If you're a pretty young girl and you're kidnapped, you'll probably even be the top story. When a famous movie star *and* one of the richest heirs in Halo City get kidnapped together, right out of their ritzy hotel room, it's not just bad news. It's big, bad, all-day, every channel news.

It's Channel-Six-in-the-Mix!-newscopters-whizzing-through-the-air, cover-of-the-*Daily-Halo*, *People*-magazine-reporters-banging-down-the-girlfriend's-door-for-a-reaction news.

When Charlie and Lisa disappeared, all that stuff happened instantly. It was like a media bomb had gone off, leaving a giant cloud over Halo City.

When I got back to my apartment, Dad and Theo were waiting for me on the couch.

"Okay," my father said as I dropped my purse on the breakfast table. "Now we're worried."

"Now we're completely spazzing out is more like it," Theo said.

"I understand. Just let me explain——" I started.

"Explain? The phone has been ringing off the hook!" Theo cut in. "First it was just the Reeds, but now it's everyone in the known world. They want to know what we think about Charlie's kidnapping!"

"This is insane, Lulu," my father said gravely.

"Well, don't worry," I told him. "Charlie is going to be rescued in no time. Daisy and I are going to get to the bottom of it."

"Ha!" my father said. "At least someone said *something* amusing today. If you think you're *getting to the bottom* of anything, you're kidding yourself, young lady. Until Charlie and Lisa are safe and sound and until everything is figured out, the only thing you and Daisy are going to be getting to the bottom of is *Madame Bovary*."

"But I finished *Madame Bovary* three days ago!" I shrieked. "She died at the end! It was totally depressing!"

"Thanks for ruining it," Theo muttered. My dad, however, wasn't paying any attention.

"Svenska and I spoke an hour ago," he said. "We've decided it's just not safe for you and Daisy to be running around town while all this is going on."

I was floored. What was my father trying to say here? Was I *grounded*? I had never been grounded before, but it didn't sound like a lot of fun, especially when there was the important business of saving my best friend at hand.

"You're letting *Svenska* give you parenting tips?" I was growing more and more agitated.

"That's not what I said," my dad argued. "I just think—"

I didn't let him finish. I threw myself face-first on the couch and began clawing at it, wailing.

"Let's not be dramatic, Lulu." My father sighed.

"Dramatic? *Dramatic?* My best friend has just been kidnapped by my *mother*! I think the situation calls for dramatics!"

"Well, maybe you're right," he said. "But sorry. I've made up my mind. It's not a punishment, Lu. I just don't want you to get kid-napped! Can you blame me for that?"

"Yes," I said.

"Don't worry. It'll be fun," Theo said. "We'll watch TV, play games, read fashion magazines—it will be just like camping!"

My father and I both looked at Theo like he was from Mars.

"Have you ever been camping?" Dad asked Theo.

"No," Theo said. "So?"

"If you'd go into the woods expecting to watch TV and read fash-ion magazines, you should probably never try it," I told him.

"Well, you know what I mean," Theo persisted. "It will be like camping but with running water and electricity. The best of both worlds!"

"I'm not feeling it," I said, still facedown on the couch.

"Well, *feel it*," Dad said. "Because that's how it's going to be. Maybe you can even start your summer assignments for school."

That was the last straw. "Are you trying to make me cry here?" I moaned.

It wasn't until I crawled into bed, exhausted, that I made good on that promise. I am not normally much of a crier. But I'm not heartless, either, no matter how much I might like to pretend otherwise. And as the events of the day—no, not the day, the whole last two *weeks*—began to sink in, I totally lost it.

Forget my mother. Seriously. Just forget her. I was completely over her predicament at this point. And forget Lisa Lincoln. No, I wasn't happy that she had been kidnapped, but she really wasn't my problem. All I cared about was Charlie. I couldn't believe how unbelievably stupid I'd been. He had been my best friend since I was four years old, and I had screwed things up so royally. Not only had I ruined our friendship, but if I hadn't been such a jerk, he would never have been hanging out with Lisa Lincoln, and he wouldn't be in all this trouble now.

In my carelessness I'd hurt his feelings *and* I'd gotten him kidnapped. I was a terrible person, and now we were both paying for it. I might never see him again.

I guess my crying was louder than I'd known, because after a few minutes, my father crept into the room and sat on the edge of my bed. He didn't say a word, just put his hand on my back and let it sit there.

I felt like such a baby. But screw it. This wasn't the time for pride. I curled into his leg and just let loose.

As the week went on, I slowly began to go crazy. There was so much going on in the outside world, and my only connection to any of it was my incessant visits from Detective Wanda, who was growing more and more frantic in her grillings as the publicity on the case intensified. When I finally spilled all the beans to her, she was grateful for the information but not grateful enough to clue me in on what *she* had discovered.

"Oh no, Lulu," she said when I asked. "I know you. As soon as I tell you where the investigation's going, you'll be out your bedroom window on a rope made from paper clips, trying to solve it yourself. For someone who says she hates girl detectives, you're certainly interested in solving crimes."

I begged, wheedled, harangued, and cajoled. Wanda remained unmoved. Eventually I just gave up and resigned myself to the fact that I wasn't going to get anything out of her. Instead I settled for taking her chocolates, which I required her to bring me every day. That was a request she could comply with.

Meanwhile, the Reed family was going understandably insane over the senseless kidnapping of their beloved only son. Charlie's big sister, Genevieve, was doing her part to bring him home by making daily televised pleas to the kidnappers for his safe return.

It's mean of me to say, and I'm not trying to imply that she didn't want her brother back, but I'm sure Genevieve didn't mind getting her mug on the national news practically every night. As an aspiring actress/model, it was good exposure.

Mr. and Mrs. Reed, on the other hand, had chosen a different tactic for rescuing Charlie. They had simply opened up their checkbooks and hired a whole team of private detectives.

If they did what they were supposed to do—namely, rescue Charlie—I wasn't going to be offended. But considering the amount of time the detectives spent being interviewed on television, I was doubtful that they were actually getting anything done.

Through it all, Theo and my father were sympathetic. Dad felt bad enough about my plight that he waited on me hand and foot. All I had to do was say the word and he was out the door to the bodega to get me ice cream or magazines or a DVD rental or whatever. Theo, on the other hand, didn't leave my side. Ever. He tried to pretend it was because he was having so much fun hanging out with me, but let's face it: Hangman isn't that fun to start with, and it loses its charm pretty quickly, no matter how amazing the company. I knew the real score. My father had assigned him the job of watching over me.

That Theo, of all people, was supposed to be my bodyguard was pretty hysterical if you thought about it. I mean, trust me, I love him, but the man is a total sissy. He's built like a hobbit—a skinny hobbit. I've beaten him at arm wrestling on more than one occasion. Seriously, I really have. So I don't know what he was supposed to do if a bunch of kidnappers came bursting through the window on a zip cord. Fight them off with a pillow? Pull me in front of him and use me as a human shield? If anything, I would probably wind up protecting *him*.

Daisy was enjoying her imprisonment even less than I was. After all, she was stuck with *Svenska*. Every day she'd call me sounding more and more despondent. "Lulu, I can't take it anymore," she whined over the phone. "Svenska's pushing me too far. It would be one thing if she'd just let me stay in my room and read or something, but she expects me to, like, play with her! Every day she has these activities for us. Yesterday we made friendship bracelets. Today it was constructing miniature doll food out of craft clay! I'm afraid to even think of what she's going to come up with next!"

Daisy and I distracted ourselves by trying to figure out what the kidnappers wanted and what they'd do next.

I know that sounds strange, trying to solve a mystery from your bedroom, but I watch PBS sometimes, and they have this woman named Miss Marple who just sits there in her parlor. In this show someone will, like, tell Miss Marple a mystery, and she'll just stay in her armchair for a while, take a sip of her tea, and then bust out with the entire solution without leaving her fussy little house. She's pretty amazing.

Daisy and I figured that if a little old lady like that could do it, so could we. Unfortunately, we weren't really getting anywhere. Daisy's theories were all too harebrained, and mine—well, they all led back to the same place: my mother.

What was her deal? I mean, I understood that she was pissed off about the state of her career, but it was totally, totally unlike her to actually *do* anything about it. Plus she had always been an intensely *a*political person. And now she was engaging in acts of art terrorism and calling threats in to gossip columnists?

Okay, that wasn't exactly *politics*, but the last time I'd seen my mother get so worked up was when Donatella took over Versace.

So something was definitely awry. Several things were, actually. As much as all the evidence pointed to the notion that Isabelle was the mastermind behind the kidnapping—there was still that phone call. The one I'd gotten right before Charlie and Lisa vanished.

My mom had only spoken one sentence, but she had almost definitely sounded like she was trying to *stop* the kidnapping.

Furthermore, stealing a statuette was one thing, but kidnapping Lisa *and* Charlie, whom she'd known since he was a baby? It just seemed like going too far.

I knew that. I did. But still, I couldn't shake a feeling that whatever was going on, it was because she was guilty. I didn't know what she was guilty *of*, exactly, but she had to be guilty of something.

I sighed to myself. No. No, she didn't. The dirty truth was that I only *wanted* her to be guilty. Because then the world would see what I knew all along—that Isabelle was a big letdown.

Yes, it was disloyal of me. Yes, she's still my mother and I'm supposed to love her no matter what. But it seems to me that there's a special category of love that is reserved just for one's family members.

The kind of love that doesn't necessarily preclude something close to hate.

Can I say that? I'm not sure. It's definitely not going to win me any Daughter of the Year prizes, but that sounds like a pretty dumb prize anyway. I'd rather win the Painfully Honest Truths for Young Ladies award.

The answer, of course, was totally obvious: Isabelle wasn't the culprit. She wasn't the Fox. I'd been barking up the wrong tree. And as much as Miss Marple makes it look otherwise, it isn't so easy to solve a mystery from your armchair or, in my case, your divan.

If nothing else, you have to get up and stretch your legs.

Charlie had rescued me once. Now it was my turn to rescue him.

If only I could come up with a plan.

The next day I was going about my business, playing an exciting game of twenty questions with Theo (I was winning). I went to my bedroom to get a pair of socks, opened up my closet, and discovered, amid the coat hangers—a human being!

I opened my mouth to scream. I was just about to let a good one loose when the person's head popped out from an old Miu Miu cardigan. It was Daisy!

I mean, it was sort of Daisy. It's a good thing I can recognize that girl anywhere; otherwise I might have killed her without thinking. She was wearing big horn-rimmed glasses, a black wig, and some kind of prosthetic nose that looked like it had been affixed with Elmer's glue.

"Don't scream," she whispered.

"Daisy," I gasped, "what are you doing here? Why are you in my *closet*? And what's with that nose? It really is *not* flattering."

"We have to talk," Daisy said urgently. "Is it safe?"

"I don't know." I glanced over my shoulder. "I told Theo I was getting a pair of socks. He's waiting for me in the living room."

"Hmmm," Daisy said. "Well, we're going to need to think of a way to get rid of him. Otherwise we're never going to get out of here."

I frowned at her. "Did I already ask you how you got *in*?"

"Your security leaves something to be desired," she said knowingly. She stepped out of the closet and brushed herself off. "Actually, I just walked in the door. I have keys, you know. No one was paying any attention. You guys were too busy watching one of those *E! True Hollywood Stories* you like so much."

"Haley Joel Osment." I nodded. "That's a good one."

"Well, I've got bad news," Daisy said. "Have you seen the *Daily Halo* today?"

"No," I said.

"Svenska tried to sneak it into the trash before I could get a look at it. But it's not good," Daisy reported. She reached into her handbag and pulled out the tabloid, which was still stained with coffee grounds and some unidentifiable produce. I grabbed it from her.

LISA AND CHARLIE, the headline screamed, DEAD MEAT AT DAWN!!!

My stomach dropped. I turned to Daisy, who was just standing there with a grim look on her face. I mean, I'm sure it would have been grim beneath the fake nose, the wig, et cetera.

Nervously I flipped through and found the article. But it turned

out that the article wasn't what was important. On the opposite
page, in huge, boldface cursive type, was the following message:

Attention, Halo city
We have been scorned long enough.
Tomorrow Charlie and Lisa die.
Yours truly,
The Fox

I turned to Daisy. "Is this serious?"

"Looks like it," she said.

I considered the situation. It was time for action. "We need a cell
phone," I said.

"I stole Svenska's this morning. I figured we might need it," Daisy
said.

She handed the phone over, and I began to type in a text message.

TICKETS FOR SECRET BEYONCÉ SHOW. ON SALE NOW! MUST BUY IN
PERSON AT THE COLISEUM. COME QUICK. WILL SELL OUT FAST.

Chances were, Theo wouldn't recognize the incoming number. He
didn't have Svenska in his phone, so I figured we'd be safe.

About thirty seconds after I pressed send, I heard excited squealing from the next room.

"What is it, Theo?" I asked, stepping out of my bedroom.

"Lulu," he said. "I have to leave for a *half hour*. It's very important. Do *not* tell your father. It will be our little secret."

"Are you sure?" I asked, making a face of disappointment. "Our game of twenty questions was just starting to get interesting!"

Theo was already halfway out the door, jamming his wallet in his back pocket. "I'll be back before you know it!" he said. "Just sit tight. Don't go anywhere."

The door slammed behind him.

I did feel a little bad, tricking Theo like this. He's a good guy, and I was going to get him in trouble with Dad. Not to mention worry him. But desperate times call for desperate measures. And you know what? I'm a teenage girl. If a teenage girl can't be expected to sneak out of the house every now and then, what is the world even coming to?

"Daisy, you can come out!" I called when the coast was clear.

She came bounding into the living room. "Nice work," she cheered.

"Thanks, but we need to hurry—it's not going to be long before Theo figures out that Beyoncé's in Saint-Tropez this week. And you and I have a friend to save."

TWELVE DAISY AND I SPRINTED

to the subway station.

"So, what's the plan, Chief?" she asked.

I turned to face her. "The plan, my dear sidekick, is to rescue Charlie and win him back."

"Wait," Daisy said. "Now you want Charlie back?"

I just grinned mysteriously. But the truth was, when I finally saw Charlie again, I was going to tell him that I had messed up royally.

If—I mean *when*—I finally saw him again, I was going to get down on my knees, tell him I had been a weak little woman, and beg him to come back to me forever and ever. It was going to be just like a Petula Clark song.

Okay, it was going to be *nothing* like a Petula Clark song. I was going to remain the upright, dignified young lady that I am and apologize for being so indecisive. Then I was going to suck up my pride and suggest that perhaps I had made a slight error in dumping him and ask if we could consider the possibility of rectifying that mistake.

The point was, I was going to get him back.

I pulled out my cell phone and turned to Daisy. "Check out this little number," I said, waving it in her face.

"What's that?" Daisy asked, squinting.

"Right before Charlie and Lisa were kidnapped, Isabelle called me. Remember?"

"Sure," Daisy said. "So?"

"So I saved the number. And I've been wondering about it all week."

"Why didn't you call it before?"

"When I was stuck in the Gulag? The Fox would have known I was on to him—or her—and I wouldn't have been able to do anything about it. Now at least we have a chance of ambushing them."

I pressed the send button and held the phone to my ear.

It rang. And rang. And rang. I held my breath.

Finally, after the sixth ring, someone picked up.

"This Sparkle?" The voice on the line was dyspeptic.

"Um, yes," I lied. "Who is this?"

"This is Contessa," croaked the woman, who sounded like she'd just finished gargling a tank full of gasoline. "This is Sparkle, right?"

"*Yes*, Contessa, this is Sparkle," I said. "Where are you?"

"Right where I said I was going to be. You got the stuff?"

"Of course I have the stuff. But I forgot where you said we were meeting."

"At the pay phone! Jackson and Ross," she snapped. "Hurry up!"
Click.

I grinned at Daisy. "We're in business," I said. "There's this woman named Contessa. She told me exactly where the pay phone is. I think she's expecting us to bring her drugs!"

"I have some Midol," Daisy suggested. "Do you think that counts?"

"Maybe if you give her the whole bottle!" I laughed. "Let's go. Jackson and Ross."

I pondered the subway and then, emboldened by my success, decided to splurge. I stuck my arm out for a taxi.

We made our way to South Halo, near the piers, where the skyscrapers and trees give way to warehouses, abandoned factories, and brown, dead patches of unclaimed grass. Hardly anyone was out on the street, and those people who were looked like they would be doing themselves a favor if they checked into a hospital. There were hardly any cars, save for a few rumbling trucks.

South Halo is not exactly the crown jewel of Halo City. Basically, it's a dump.

"You sure this is where you want to get out?" the cabdriver asked skeptically. "Does your mother know you're here?"

"We don't have mothers," I said. "We're orphans."

I guess that made it okay, because we paid our money and he drove off without another word.

In all my excitement over finding a lead, I hadn't stopped to think about how we were walking right into danger. I hadn't even brought my old spatula with me for protection.

There was one thing to be relieved about, however, and that was the fact that no one was waiting for us at the rusty pay phone on the corner. Contessa must have gotten sick of waiting around for Sparkle. Or maybe Sparkle had even showed up—though neither of them, in my imagination, was really the reliable type.

"So, here we are," Daisy said.

"Yep," I observed.

I surveyed the desolate landscape. There wasn't a lot to see—nothing particularly suspicious. Or rather, *everything* was suspicious, so it was hard to pick out anything specific. I mean, if you see a dirty van with tinted windows, you think, *That looks like a criminal's vehicle*, and you break into it and hopefully whatever you're looking for will be inside. If you see, like, ten dirty vans with tinted windows, parked up and down the block, with abandoned buildings everywhere and every one of them looking more like a hideout than the last, well, then you're just in a really bad neighborhood and there's not a lot you can do.

"I feel a little uneasy," Daisy said. "We're sitting ducks."

"Not for long. It's time for a stakeout," I told her. "Let's find something we can hide behind."

Daisy and I peered up and down the block. Usually there's some kind of shrub around when I need it. But in this neighborhood, vegetation was in short supply. There *weren't* any bushes. There was an anemic tangle of weeds that sort of resembled a bush in terms of basic shape, but it really wasn't appropriate for hiding. Instead I spotted two lone metal trash cans. We hid behind those.

We waited. Nothing happened. We waited some more.

"Are you sure we're in the right place?" Daisy asked.

"Just wait," I said. "I bet something will happen."

And then a pair of hands grabbed us from behind.

We screamed.

"Just what do you two think you're doing?!" Svenska shrieked, dragging us out from behind our spot.

"Svenska?!" Daisy cried.

"Don't call me that," her mother snapped. "I don't know what you two are up to, but it looks devilish to me. If my mother had ever caught *me* hiding in a trash can . . . Well, I just don't even know where to begin."

"We weren't hiding *in* trash cans," Daisy said. "We were hiding *behind* trash cans."

"Well, last time I checked, good husbands don't go looking for wives at the dump," Svenska said. "Come on. You two are going straight home before you get kidnapped like those friends of yours." She narrowed her eyes. "Or *worse*."

She grabbed Daisy by the collar like a puppy and pulled her to her feet.

I didn't move. Svenska scowled at me.

"Well, Miss Trixie Belden?"

I was sweating, and it wasn't from the weather. Svenska terrifies me. I had never tried to stand up to her before—but there was a first time for everything.

"Sorry," I told her, not quite stuttering. "I'm staying exactly where I am. Our friends are missing. I have a responsibility to them."

Svenska opened her mouth, then closed it again. Then she opened it and closed it again. Daisy covered her eyes with her hand, terrified of the hellfire that was surely about to be unleashed. But it didn't come.

"Suit yourself, fancy pants!" Svenska sniffed. And she and Daisy were off, headed for the subway. Daisy snuck a surreptitious glance over her shoulder and waved a feeble goodbye before Svenska slapped her hand down. She looked like she was about to cry. And I was all by myself.

I sat there for the next hour behind that trash can, feeling more despondent with each passing minute. Nothing was happening. *Was* I in the right place?

I had to be, I reasoned. My mother had called me from that pay phone, so I kept my eyes trained there.

I let my mind wander while I waited. I was just beginning to mull over other routes of investigation, when, finally, there was some action across the street.

First I heard voices. Then, exiting the door of one of the warehouses came a procession of blond, middle-aged tarts, all wearing black strappy tanks and what looked to be imitation Ugg boots. Each was hauling a black plastic trash bag, packed to the gills.

"You got everything, ladies?" the first blonde, who seemed to be the leader, called out. I had seen her before, I realized with a start. She had been one of the hotel "maids" that night with Lisa Lincoln.

Then it dawned on me—this faux maid had looked familiar even then, and suddenly I knew why. I had seen her on TV—playing Scooter Rasmussen, the ditzy sister on *Relatively Speaking*. That show was so old that I barely remembered it, but I could now see her much-younger face clearly in my mind, going around and around through a revolving door during the opening credits. It's funny the weird things that you have floating around in your brain without even knowing it.

"Jeannette Franklin," I murmured to myself. "That's Jeannette Franklin."

She looked up. Oops. I guess I hadn't been as quiet as I thought.

"What was that?" she asked her cronies.

They all shrugged, like they didn't know what she was talking about.

"Someone just said my name," Jeannette Franklin insisted. She looked around and then headed straight in my direction. I held my breath and tried to make myself as small as humanly possible. It seemed to work. She got about five feet away from my trash can hideout, then turned around without spotting me. I breathed a (totally silent) sigh of relief.

Jeanette's crew followed her to—you guessed it—one of the many dirty vans parked on the street. They passed right by my trash can, and I squinted to make out their faces. It wasn't just Jeanette/Scooter who was familiar.

There was Gina Gladstone from *You Crack Me Up!* There was Trinks Arnold from *The Truth About Amy.* There was the chesty life-guard from *Coast Guard Jamboree.* Even the faces that I couldn't quite place, I knew I recognized from somewhere.

The pattern had made itself clear. All of these women were old-time TV stars!

Trinks slammed the sliding door of the van, and the van sped off down the street.

Slowly I crept out of my hiding spot and moved toward the warehouse. I hung back when I reached the door.

Should I knock? I wondered. It didn't seem right to knock on the door of a crime lair. But what choice did I have? If Daisy was here, she'd just climb in a window or pick the lock. But on my own, I was feeling slightly more cautious. I reached out and rapped at the door.

There was no answer. Thank goodness. Feeling much better, I turned the handle and went for it.

My anxiety was wasted. When I stepped inside the warehouse, I found only a huge, cavernous nothing. Just a dark, dank, cobwebby cement cave, and that was it. The only sign that people had even been here were the empty Diet Pepsi cans strewn everywhere—and I do mean *everywhere*. There were hundreds of them, lying around like carcasses. I didn't know exactly who had been living here, but I seriously hoped they saw the dentist on a regular basis. That stuff will rot your teeth if you're not careful.

I wandered around, sifting through the detritus. Nothing. I guessed that this place could at some point have been some sort of headquarters. The former sitcom stars with the trash bags might have been here to gather up the last of any incriminating evidence.

Drat. I'd hit another dead end.

Until—in the far corner of the warehouse I noticed a little hatch built into the floor.

A trapdoor!

Since no one was around to see me, I danced a private, deeply embarrassing jig. Trapdoors always have something exciting behind them in the movies. And let's face it—my life might as well have been a movie at this point.

I pulled open the hatch and climbed down. It was pitch black.

Feeling incredibly Boy Scout–like and well prepared, I reached into my handbag and pulled out a teensy flashlight. Man, I was good! The batteries even worked! I clicked it on to discover that I was standing in a windowless, bathroom-sized compartment with a small, sagging cot in the corner. It smelled like mildew. I let my beam drift up and down the walls and across the floor of the cell, hoping to spot something that would give me a clue as to who had been here. There was nothing except for a tangled-up cable of nylon rope.

Ew. *That* was comforting.

You know how it is when you can't find what you're looking for. You look up and down for it, going crazy, accusing innocent people of theft-slash-tomfoolery, and then your dad says, "Did you check under the bed?" and naturally you lie and say yes (in a petulant tone) because you know for *sure* that there is no way it could possibly be under the bed and how could he have such a stupid notion, and then, finally, when you're totally over it, you think, *Well, what the heck,* so you check under the bed, and there it is, whatever was missing, and it's been there all along, and you feel like an utter tool.

Maybe I should check under the bed, I thought.

Gingerly I got onto my hands and knees. I scrunched up my nose and stuck my head under the cot, shining my flashlight back and forth.

Aha! A piece of paper lay there, jammed up against the wall.

I reached under on my stomach and fished it out. When I retrieved it and unfolded it, I couldn't have been more surprised.

It was a photograph.

At the beach, in the surf, a seven-year-old in her swimsuit, raising her arms to the sky. It was me—in the picture that Lisa Lincoln had told me about; the one she'd said that my mother never went anywhere without.

Well, she was certainly without it now—wherever she was.

Before that, though, she must have been here. I looked around again, suddenly recalibrating my opinions. Had my mother been sleeping here? I looked down at the nylon rope on the floor. A horrifying thought dawned on me.

Had she been *tied up* here?

Goose bumps crawled up my forearms. I really *had* gotten everything wrong.

I stuffed the photo into the pocket of my sweats and scrambled back up the ladder. I needed to get out of there as quickly as possible. I was starting to get an idea of what had been going on here, and it wasn't pretty.

Still, if I was going to do this right, I had to do one more sweep, just to make sure I hadn't missed anything. I was on the main floor, sifting through a mountain of soda cans, when it caught my eye: a business card. It was plastered to the bottom of a can, fixed firmly in place by what must be the stickiest and most disgusting substance known to man—petrified diet soda.

The card had practically become one with the aluminum, but, using every ounce of my own girlish might, I managed to pry it off and flip it over.

There was an address. There was a phone number. There was a name.

And the name was Fletcher Rose.

THIRTEEN THE JIG WAS UP.

Isn't that what detectives always say when they've found the culprit?

If Fletcher Rose—that tragic little homunculus—thought he could kidnap my mother and my boyfriend, not to mention my celebrity frienemy, Lisa Lincoln, I felt sorry for him.

Not to speak in the third person (tacky!), but Lulu Dark is not a girl to be trifled with. I'd proved it before and I would prove it again.

The home address on the card was 1 Persimmon Square, one of the trendiest of all addresses in Halo City. It's a huge black tower near my high school in the Orchard District, where all the streets are named for different types of fruit. I didn't have a plan, but sometimes it's better just to play it by ear anyway. Instinct counts. All I knew was that I was going to bust over to Fletcher's apartment, confront him, and get my friends back.

I wasn't afraid of him. I was at least six inches taller!

The only problem was getting there. Exiting the warehouse, I cast my eyes up and down the block in search of cabs, then realized with a sinking feeling that cabs just didn't come to this part of town without a reason. It wasn't like the rest of Halo City, where there are like ten taxis on every block. Here you were lucky if you saw any car at all. The subway wasn't too far away, but that would take *forever.* It would take at least three transfers to get anywhere near the Orchard District. I just didn't have time for that.

And then, as if it had been sent by God himself, I saw a lonely city bus rumbling down the street.

Oh, Halo City Department of Public Transportation, I thought, bursting into a sprint, *thank you, thank you, thank you!*

The bus was stopped at a red light when I finally caught up and began frantically pounding on the door. I know bus drivers aren't allowed to make unscheduled stops, but I was desperate. After a few seconds of banging there was a hiss and a pop, and the door opened up. I scrambled aboard.

"Do you go to the Orchard District?" I wheezed to the driver, a portly woman in a blue uniform, whose name tag read FRANCIE. She did not look pleased.

"Nope," she said.

"Ummm . . . please?" I begged.

"Get on or get off." She sighed. "I have a schedule. This bus goes straight up to Halo Park."

That did me no good whatsoever.

"I'm sorry, but you don't understand. This is an emergency!"

"Not my problem," she said. "Get on or get off."

The passengers on the bus weren't having it either.

"We have places to go!" a decrepit old man in the front row

yelled at me, waving his dog-eared copy of *THEY Weekly* to demonstrate his rage.

"This isn't a limousine service!" screamed a woman with a baby. She too had a copy of *THEY*, which her baby was perusing with as much interest as an infant can probably muster.

On the cover of the magazine, naturally, was Lisa Lincoln.

A thought occurred to me. A pretty excellent one, if I did say so myself.

"Excuse me, everyone. I don't want to waste your time during this busy day," I addressed the crowd, "but what if I told you that *you* could help rescue Lisa Lincoln?"

There was a collective gasp, followed by a flurry of murmurs.

"I'm Lulu Dark," I told them. "Friend of Lisa and Charlie Reed. I was photographed with Lisa just the other day."

That's the girl from the papers! I heard people whispering.

So they recognized me! Sort of. It was funny to think of myself as a celebrity—and I was sure everyone would forget all about me in a matter of weeks—but on that particular day my association with the Lisa Lincoln was as important to these people as their transit cards.

"You really know Lisa Lincoln?" the bus driver asked.

"Yes, Francie," I said, "I do. And if I don't rescue her *right now*, they are totally going to kill her!"

Everyone on the bus gasped. But the bus driver was torn.

"I gotta stick to my route," she said, resigned.

I turned from her and addressed the bus again. "Come on, guys.

Lisa Lincoln needs your help. Are you with me?" Again there was chatter.

I'm not sure who started the chant, but it began softly, then grew. In a matter of seconds everyone on the bus had joined in. "Lisa Lincoln! Lisa Lincoln! Lisa Lincoln!"

"Please, Francie?" I asked the driver one more time. "It's a matter of life and death!"

"Okay." She sighed yet again. "But you better be the one to explain this to my supervisor." And with that, she turned the bus around and we shot like a bullet up the deserted avenue.

Five minutes later we were idling on Persimmon Square, right in front of my destination.

"This is where you're going?"

"Yep," I said. "Thank you so much!"

I was about to disembark when I looked out the window at the dark, imposing tower. The doorman for the building stood inside, peering through the glass door with a look of suspicion.

"What's wrong, Lulu?" the lady with the baby called.

"Well," I said. "I bet you guys could all meet Lisa if you helped me with just one more thing. . . ."

"Are you ready?" I asked a moment later. "On your mark!" I called. "Get set! *Charge!*"

Francie swung the bus doors open and I bounded off the bus with about fifty excitable public transit riders close on my heels. We raced up to the building and through the doors, where my companions mobbed the poor doorman.

While he struggled to maintain order amid the chaos, I slipped right by him and into the stairwell.

There really is nothing like an unruly mob of bus riders to create a diversion.

Fletcher Rose's apartment was on the twelfth floor of the building, which is quite a jog even if you're in shape. Unfortunately, I'm not in shape. Even during a normal summer I spend between sixty and ninety-eight percent of my time engaged in sedentary activities. And this was not a normal summer. The most exercise I'd gotten in the past few weeks was from running back and forth across the room to the TV to change the channels when I'd misplaced the remote control.

By the time I reached the top of the stairs, I was completely out of breath.

Out of breath with no plan. What was I going to say to Fletcher? "Give me my mother back or I'll sweat on you"?

I hunched over at the stairwell door to catch my breath and took all of two seconds to actually think about the situation.

Until then it hadn't occurred to me to wonder why Fletcher was doing all this. Everything—from what Jaycee had told me about the Fox, to my mother's speech at the Halo Awards, to the newspaper ad just that day—suggested some kind of birdbrained, pseudo-feminist motive behind his antics. But why should Fletcher Rose give a crap? Was he just . . . sensitive?

You never know, but it seemed more likely that it was all just a smoke screen for another motive.

What, though? What *was* Fletcher's motive? If I could figure it out, it might help me crack him.

Unfortunately, it wasn't the time to be pondering such questions. The only thing I could be sure of when it came to Fletcher Rose was that he was a sleazy, corpulent little Hollywood pipsqueak. And if there's one thing I know about these Hollywood types—corpulent or otherwise—it's that flattery will get you everywhere.

So I did what I had to do. I took a deep breath and put on my most obsequious smile. I knocked on the door. After a few moments it cracked open. I saw a beady eye staring at me.

"Lulu Dark?" Fletcher wheezed. "What are you doing here?" He sounded nervous. Well, that was a good sign, at least.

I fluttered my eyelashes. "Fletcher," I cooed. "I know about everything. And I think it's *amazing.*"

"What are you talking about?" he whispered.

"Oh, don't be so modest," I said. "You don't need to be secretive with me. I'm your number-one fan. I would never tell. I'm on your side. I want to help."

"I'm confused," he said. "You—you like my movies?"

I stretched my arm across the door frame and leaned in. "Let's just say," I whispered, "that I think you're a real *fox.*"

Fletcher groaned. "Oh God. Come in. Let's clear this up now."

He opened the door and I trotted inside, trying to ignore the butterflies in my stomach. I really hoped I wasn't totally screwing up, marching blithely into the lair of a kidnapper and supposed soon-to-be murderer. I know, I know. It sounds like a bad move. But what else was I supposed to do? *I wanted my boyfriend back.*

Fletcher's apartment was, naturally, gorgeous, and tempted as I was to ask for the tour, I really didn't have time for an impromptu *Cribs* session. Instead I scanned the place, looking for signs of prisoners. *If I were a kidnapper,* I was thinking, *where would I hide two starlets and the heir to a shoelace fortune?*

It was a huge, sparkling loft, and whoever had decorated it had clearly been going the minimalist route—all glass and metal and bare surfaces. Through the panoramic window the Halo City skyline looked like it had been sketched in highlighter.

Unfortunately, the place was so sleek and spotless that there wasn't even room to hide a ballpoint pen, much less several unruly people. I don't know what I was expecting. A big cage in the corner? There wasn't one.

Fletcher was sweating and kneading his palms together. His nylon jogging suit was rumpled and only half zipped from the waist, revealing a nauseating pelt of matted chest fur. Double puke. His eyes were bloodshot. It looked like he hadn't slept in days.

"Sit down, Lulu," Fletcher said. "Let's talk. I think you've got the wrong idea."

I tossed my hair and tried to maximize my cleavage by pushing my biceps against my boobs.

"Of course," I said. "I can't wait to hear all about everything. I'm so impressed with what you've accomplished."

"Uh-huh," he grunted. "I know what you're thinking, Lulu, but I'm not the Fox, so just cool your jets."

"What a kidder!" I said, plopping myself onto a leather sofa that was as long as three minivans stretched end to end. "A *handsome* kidder, though."

His right eyelid twitched. A sure sign of someone with something to hide.

"Listen, do you want a drink or something?" he asked. "Let's talk about things rationally."

If ever there was a time for a stiff one, this was it. On the other hand, it didn't seem like I needed to add to my problems by becoming a teenage alcoholic.

"I'll have a ginger ale," I said. "Straight up, on the rocks."

"C-coming right up," he stuttered, and shuffled over to the enormous, stainless steel refrigerator. At a loss for anything better to do, I prayed that my Mata Hari act would work. In normal life I was more of a goofball than a smooth seductress, but I'd seen enough Sandra Bullock movies to know how that it's possible for the coltish zany type to have a certain sultry je ne sais quoi if she only uses the right moves.

I puckered my lips and twirled my hair around my pinky finger. I *think* that's how it's done. Right?

I was starting to feel like a real, practiced sexpot when I glanced over to the kitchen island and noticed that Fletcher wasn't there. *Huh?*

I looked up.

Uh-oh.

Is *uh-oh* a strong enough word to use when you have a gun pointed at your skull? Probably not. But I've been warned to avoid cursing as much as possible in order for my adventures to retain their family-friendly rating.

Fletcher Rose was standing above me, gripping a pistol in both hands. It was trained on me. He was shaking.

"I don't want to hurt you," he said.

I was no longer feeling so cucumber cool.

"If you don't want to hurt me, then put that thing down!" I squealed. "Are you crazy?"

Pardon me for being Queen Obvious.

"Just get up, Lulu," he said. "You're the one who put me in this position."

That seemed debatable, but I wasn't going to argue with him on such a minor point. Not having any other choice, I stood up slowly, my heart pounding, and put my hands over my head. He hadn't told me to put my hands up, but it seemed like the appropriate action.

"What do you want me to do?" I asked.

"Um," Fletcher said, eyes darting back and forth. "Turn around." It was totally obvious that he was making this all up as he went along, but I turned around anyway. "Do you want me to, like, go somewhere or something?" I asked.

"The bathroom!" Fletcher said, improvising again. "Go lie on the bathroom floor. And stay there unless you want your head blown off. Or whatever."

"Fine," I said. "Just tell me which way the bathroom is."

I felt a sharp, cold prodding between my shoulder blades. I jumped. Maybe this guy actually *did* mean business. I let him lead me to the bathroom, praying that he didn't pull the trigger by accident. This fellow was pretty jumpy, after all. One stray muscle spasm on his part and my lavender velour jogging suit was going to be a decidedly different color.

Fletcher shoved me into the bathroom and slammed the door behind me. I heard him fiddling with the doorknob. He was locking me in! Personally, I never heard of a bathroom that locked from the outside, but I guess fancy apartments are specially tricked out for hostage situations. You know the fabulously wealthy—they're always pulling wacky crimes!

"Just stay in there and you won't get hurt," Fletcher snapped from the other side of the door. "Give yourself a manicure or something. Isn't that what teenage girls like to do?"

Oh *no*, he didn't. It's one thing to threaten me with a loaded gun. It's another to be condescending!

Whatever, I told myself. *Just let it go. After all, Isabelle, Charlie, and Lisa's lives are at stake.*

"Come on, Fletcher," I shouted back, trying to goad him. "You've got me where you want me. Isn't this the part where you're supposed to tell me your whole plan? I can't do anything about it now. You might as well satisfy my curiosity and come clean."

"You're really dense for a detective," he said. "I'm not sure how it's escaped a sharp tool like you, but I don't *have* a plan. I'm not the Fox, and you're totally barking up the wrong tree."

Sometimes being Lulu Dark really sucks. Not only do I seem to be plagued by criminals, but they're the most scatterbrained, least effective criminals of all time. How are you supposed to foil the plan of a villain who hasn't even bothered to formulate one?

One way or another, I was going to have to try.

"Come on, Fletcher." I kept up the pressure. "I heard you in the haunted house at Corona Beach. You said you had something in store for my mother."

On the other side of the door Fletcher laughed a dry, humorous laugh.

"In *store* for her?" he asked. "*My* plan was to edit *Hell Circus* so that Isabelle looked like the worst actress in the world. It served her right after taking Fiona's part. But I have nothing to do with the kidnapping or any of this!"

"I'd be more convinced if you hadn't just threatened me with a gun and locked me in the bathroom," I said.

I could hear frustrated wheezing, even through the door. "Could you just . . . just *shut up*?" Fletcher sputtered. "I need to figure out what I'm doing here."

I heard his footsteps retreating from the doorway. Frantically I glanced around the bathroom, searching for something that I could make into a useful tool. At a loss, I grabbed a toothbrush. I had recently read an article about how inmates grind down the handles of toothbrushes into sharp little points to make deadly shivs.

Sadly, I had neither the time nor the grinding implement to execute such a plan.

Argh! I hurled the toothbrush into the toilet in pure frustration. Fletcher Rose would be sorry when he got infected gums.

Just then I heard muffled talking in the other room. I plastered my ear to the door, trying to make out what was being said. It was no use. I couldn't understand a word.

I glanced around again. Aha! A drinking glass was sitting on the sink. I grabbed it up and held it to the door. I pressed my ear against it, listening carefully. Amazingly, the trick worked! It amplified the volume of everything that was happening in the next room.

"I don't know what you want me to do, *Mom*," Fletcher was saying. "She just showed up here, and . . ."

Mom. He had to be talking to Fiona Greer.

Fiona Greer. Waittaminute.

My thoughts spun back to the Halo Awards. There had been an important moment, I think . . . something my father had said.

Or *almost* said before I'd cut him off.

"She and I had quite a time. . . . They used to call her Fiona the . . ."

Oh my God. Could it be? Had it been right there in front of me all along?

"They used to call her . . . *Fiona the Fox*," I finished my father's sentence.

I could have smacked myself. But I didn't.

"No, Mom," Fletcher was whining. "I'm not going to kill her! This is just crazy."

Another pause.

"Yes, I know she'd be dead already if it weren't for her stupid mother," he continued, "but I'm not going to commit a crime here!"

Wait a minute. What did Fletcher just say?

"Mom, no. You've got to give me a better idea."

Okay, so Fletcher wasn't going to kill me. That was good. Nonetheless, things were not looking up for Mom, Charlie, and Lisa.

Fiona was obviously completely off-the-chain crazy, and she had my loved ones in her clutches.

Fletcher paused.

"No, I'm not going to send her to Farmer's Island. There's no way I'm going to let you have her, the way you're acting. I mean, if nothing else, it would totally ruin my career. . . ."

All right. This was getting terribly old. If Fletcher wasn't going to kill me, why was I waiting around? I had nothing to be afraid of. So I just started screaming.

"Hold on, Mom," Fletcher said. "Now she's screaming at the top of her lungs."

He opened the door. "Could you please shut up?" he demanded. "This is, like, a very stressful situation, and you're not helping."

"No, I'm not," I said. I squeezed past him and out of his apartment without looking back. My instincts had been right. He didn't follow. And now I knew where I was going.

FOURTEEN MY HEAD WAS

spinning as I left 1 Persimmon Square and hailed a cab. I had so much to think about that I didn't even know where to start.

Normally I would have called my therapist, Dr. Adele Moskowitz, for an emergency session. Unfortunately, she was vacationing in the Pyrenees with her handsome husband and their adopted triplets, Hansel, Greta, and Ping-Li.

In a poor substitute for the counsel of a trained professional, I pulled a scrap of paper out of my purse and started to make a list. I had discovered recently that as stupid as it seems, a list can actually be very useful for getting your head back in the game.

Here is what I wrote:

THINGS TO PONDER IN THE NEXT HALF HOUR

1. How to rescue Mom, Charlie, and Lisa Lincoln. Plan necessary or play it by ear?

2. What is going on re the Fox, etc.? What is Fiona Greer's deal? How can I get the better of her?

3. When I rescue Charlie, will he be my boyfriend again?
4. Is my mother perhaps not such a bad person after all?
5. What did Fletcher mean when he said that if it weren't for Isabelle, I'd be dead already?

Those were a lot of questions. As I rode toward my destination, my mind kept returning to the final two items.

Obviously Isabelle had pulled that little stunt at the Halo Awards in the name of the Fox. But why? I mean, yes, Isabelle is crazy, but I'd known from the beginning that this kind of thing just wasn't her style.

Could it be that Isabelle hadn't had a choice? Was it possible that the Fox had blackmailed Mom into joining her?

That made sense. But how could Isabelle have been blackmailed? The woman has nothing to hide. Her life is an open book!

My mind whirred.

I thought about the way my mother had crept into town and hadn't told me she was coming.

I thought about how nervous she'd seemed in her trailer when I visited her on set and how anxious she'd seemed to get rid of me.

I remembered our missed date at the café.

And I thought of what Fletcher Rose had said: "She'd be dead already if it weren't for her stupid mother."

I felt a swelling in my chest.

My mom *was* avoiding me, I thought. But maybe it was for a good reason. Maybe it was because Fiona Greer had blackmailed Mom into helping her—by threatening to hurt *me*?

I swallowed. I had been so quick to jump to conclusions that I hadn't even thought about the possibility that Isabelle could have a shred of maternal instinct.

But something was still missing. Sure, they could have black-mailed Isabelle, but what was the point of that? Why did Fiona want her rival, Icy Inga, to be a member of her little group so badly anyway?

Could it be that Fiona the Fox still hated my mother and was try-ing to get her in trouble? It was possible. After all, this wasn't just a vendetta; it was, like, twenty years of pure resentment. That kind of thing is enough to make anyone go nuts.

Fiona must have figured she could kill two birds with one stone—proving a point while having her old nemesis take the fall. At the very least she could have ruined my mother's career.

The ironic part, of course, was that Isabelle had become more in demand than ever. Jaycee Frost had told me so. Fiona was probably *fuming* that Mom was getting the notoriety that should have been hers.

The time for list making was over. The cab slid to a stop at my destination. I handed the cabbie a wad of bills and stepped out into the summer evening. A cool breeze hit my face, blowing in from Dagger Bay.

There, floating off in the distance, was Farmer's Island—the place that I'd heard Fletcher Rose mention on the phone with Fiona.

Although it was pleasantly warm out, I felt a chill run up my spine. This was where it was all going to go down.

Farmer's Island, in the middle of Dagger Bay, is one of the most, you know, *historical* places in Halo City. It's also one of the freakiest. When I was growing up, my father used to love telling me that it was where they sent intractable little girls who were too disobedient for their own good. He found that hilarious. As an eight-year-old, I found it straight-up terrifying. Once I was older and learned more about the island, it actually scared me even more. For one thing, it turned out that my dad wasn't just teasing me. It was actually kind of true.

The island is the site of the oldest mental hospital in Halo City— the Farmer Sanitarium for Deranged and Insane Ladies. It has been shut down for as long as anyone can remember, I mean, since before my parents and probably even their parents were born, but the huge ivy-covered building still stands out there on that tiny little island in the bay. You can see it driving on the highway out of the city, looming over the water.

It doesn't look like hospitals look nowadays. It doesn't look like a shopping mall or a high school. It's gray and crumbling, with turrets and spires and narrow, pointy little windows. Maybe that almost sounds cute to you, like a nice old cat lady could live there or some-thing. But no. It's not cute. Every time you look at it, it seems like there should be a crack of thunder and a bolt of lightning, like in an old monster movie.

Back in the day, like around the turn of the century and up until World War I, Farmer's Island was where you got sent if you were an insane lady. Unfortunately for ladies everywhere, people always seem to have messed-up standards about what constitutes insanity in the female. It was especially bad back then. Pretty much anything that *I* would call "interesting," they would have called "deranged." I mean, if she'd been alive in those days, Daisy would have been carted straight to Farmer's Island and stuck in a straitjacket faster than she could tie her own shoes. (Yes, she does have trouble tying her own shoes sometimes, but that's not my point.)

The thing was, if the women weren't actually insane when they got there, it didn't take long for them to get that way once they were locked up. There are all these stories about the different ways the women would kill themselves just to get out of that hospital. Strangling themselves to death with their own hands, stabbing themselves with knitting needles, banging their heads against the walls until their skulls cracked open—you name it.

The most famous "patient" there was the silent film star Irma Cole, who was locked up for life basically just because she was sort of a slut. She later committed suicide. They say that if you stand on the shore under a full moon, you can still hear her screaming. I believe it.

When I got to the promenade at Dagger Bay, it was around seven o'clock. It was still fairly light out, but the sky was turning that shade of blue that only exists in the summertime, when it isn't day anymore but not it's not quite night yet either.

Other times of the year I guess that's called evening, but in June it's something different that I can't quite put my finger on. There in that strange, warm light I tried to figure out how I was going to get out to the hospital.

Did I mention that Farmer's Island is totally off-limits to the public these days? They used to have tours that went there, but over the years one too many people died from falling from the famous spiral staircase in the front hall or from tumbling over one of the many balconies. The insurance got to be too much, and just like that, it was closed down. There's not even any good way of getting there anymore: no ferries, nothing. I was in a pickle.

I stared out at the island, trying to come up with a viable mode of transportation. I racked my brain, trying to think of alternatives to the obvious. Helicopter? Hitching a ride on the back of a friendly dolphin? Those were the best ideas I could come up with. But really, there was no getting around it. If I wanted to get there, it was going to be by boat.

And there was only one kind of boat available: rowboat, which you could rent for ten dollars on the boardwalk.

The last time I was in a rowboat was when I was about five years old, and my dad had done all the work. I had no idea how to pilot one of those things other than recalling a vague rumor that the process involved something called an "oar." I glanced out at the other boaters, sailing through the water. How hard could it be? Rowboats were invented practically in dinosaur times. If they were able to do it in the olden days, before they could even look up instructions on the Internet, it must not take *too* much sophistication. Right?

I wandered (with purpose) over to the boat rental kiosk by the french fry stand and plunked down my cash, casting my eyes downward and avoiding the rental guy's gaze, just in case he recognized me as that girl from the kidnapping! Luckily he was about a thousand years old and probably hadn't watched television since *Lawrence Welk* went off the air. He didn't pay me the slightest mind.

So five minutes later I had my boat and was flailing around on open water with less than no clue what to do. I was slapping the surface of Dagger Bay with the oars, splashing around everywhere and generally making a huge fool of myself. What I was *not* doing was making headway toward the island. When I managed to go anywhere at all, it was just to send my vessel in a tight, pointless little circle.

This wasn't going to work. I gauged the distance to the island and wondered whether I could swim it.

Forget that. That water looked cold; plus I'm not going to be qualifying for the Olympics anytime soon—unless they invent new categories for indolence or telling tales out of school.

But as un-athletic as I may be, there comes a time when you just have to buckle down and make it happen. Your mother and your best friend being held and possibly tortured in an abandoned mental hospital is a prime example of one of those times. So finally, after about twenty minutes of experimenting, I started to figure out a few tricks. It all had to do with coordination, a concept that had heretofore been completely foreign to me. If you paddled *one* oar, you started to turn. If you paddled the other one, you'd turn in the other direction. But if you managed, improbably, to get your arms to work together enough so that you sort of moved them both at the same exact time, you would start to creep forward. It was kind of like a video game, except that it wasn't much fun and it made my biceps feel like they were made from noodles. I reminded myself that I wasn't there to have fun. I was there to save the day.

I rowed and rowed, feeling like I was getting nowhere. But slowly Farmer's Island began to grow on the horizon. I was making progress.

It took close to an hour and a half. When I finally slid the boat onto the shore, the sun was setting. Though I wanted to collapse on the rocky shore and take a nap, I knew that wasn't an option. I had to figure out what was going on and find cover before anyone inside one of the many windows or garrets noticed that there was a boat on the shore and a Lulu Dark wandering around the island.

Staying as low to the ground as I could, I surveyed the scene.

The island itself was just a hunk of boulder rising out of the bay. No grass, no trees, no nothing—just jagged, unforgiving rock. The hospital seemed like a natural extension of that landscape—more rough silver-gray harshness, constructed from rotting shingles and clapboard. The only hint of color was in the deep green spiderweb of vines clinging to the walls. All in all, it wasn't an inviting sight.

Luckily for me, the rugged terrain of the rock—with its rough peaks and valleys—provided a certain amount of cover. So when I saw movement suddenly on the periphery of my vision, I dropped to my stomach, hiding in a crevice of boulder and praying that I hadn't been noticed by whoever was walking around.

When I was pretty sure that I hadn't been discovered, I peered up, to see two women stomping across the grounds a few hundred feet away.

I wasn't surprised that one of them was the inimitable Jeannette Franklin, looking just as pinched as ever. I *was* slightly surprised—not to mention freaked out—by the fact that she was carrying a loaded crossbow. Like I've said before, those actresses really tend to overdo it with the theatrics. But whatever. The real shock was the other woman.

Striding along next to Jeanette Franklin was Trish Archer, Lisa Lincoln's bodyguard! In her arms she was cradling a shotgun, which she swept in a smooth arc ahead of her as she patrolled.

I sucked in a breath. That traitor! No wonder it had been so easy for Charlie and Lisa to get snatched. There had been a mole. I couldn't believe it hadn't occurred to me before.

In the distance I could just make out the sounds of their voices. I strained to hear what they were talking about, but before I could get to really concentrating, I jumped. My cell phone was ringing.

Crap! I had forgotten to turn it off!

If anyone ever writes a handbook for reluctant amateur sleuths, rule number one should be: put your phone on silent before infiltrating the enemy's lair.

Frantically I dug through my purse, feeling for it. Key chain . . . gum . . . toothbrush . . . flashlight . . . whistle . . . Aha!

I pulled my phone out and answered it just to make the noise stop.

"Hello?" I whispered.

"Lulu?" It was Daisy.

"I can't talk," I said, glancing around to make sure I hadn't been spied. "I'm deep in it."

"Where are you?" she asked.

"Farmer's Island," I said. "Now—"

"Great," Daisy chirped. "I've always wanted to see what it's like there. I'll hitch a boat ride!"

"Daisy!" I hissed. But she was already gone.

I looked up. Jeannette and Trish were still oblivious to my presence, thank God. They were walking away from me on the beach, heading off into the distance. Without standing, I scurried along to keep up, doing that funny little crab walk that you always see them do in movies about boot camp. I didn't want to lose them. For one thing, I figured I would be safer for now if I kept them within my sight.

My knees were starting to get pretty beat up from scooting along on the rocky ground. If I didn't give the crawling a rest soon, I'd never be able to wear shorts or miniskirts again!

Thankfully, before my legs became scarred beyond the point of return, Trish and Jeanette came to a small metal door in the side of the sanitarium and marched inside. I debated whether to follow them or not. But while I was still making up my mind, I received a sign. There, growing lonely in a funny little irregularity in the wall, I noticed a medium-sized leafy shrub. Perfect! It was just the right size to hide behind. I'd be able to bide my time there for as long as I needed.

I rose to my feet and scrambled to the wall, diving straight into the bush. I didn't care that I got a mouthful of leaves. Really, I was starting to feel like I should just carry a little potted plant with me wherever I went, along with my mace, my whistle, and my flashlight, in case I need some emergency foliage.

I wasn't hiding for long. After two minutes, tops, the women re-emerged.

"That should hold her for a while," Trish said.

"Just as long as she doesn't interfere with the Fox's plans. After those kids are cut up, we can figure out what to do with her. I can't believe the Fox was so interested in her in the first place. What's the big deal? She was never even all that famous. *Relatively Speaking* was number one for three seasons, you know. I couldn't even name one thing that *she*'s done."

There was only one person they could be talking about: my mom.

Well, I *was* there to rescue her, right? She had to be behind that door. When the women were out of sight, I pushed through and ventured inside the building, nervous about what I would find.

I didn't have to look far. There, in the corner of a small, nondescript room, was Isabelle, bound to a wooden chair with a gag in her mouth.

It was pretty hard seeing my mother like that. Her hair was matted and her face was wan and strung out, like she hadn't slept in a week. Her head just hung there, limp, her eyes bloodshot and caked with a week's worth of crust. As soon as she saw me, the expression of despair on her face began to fade.

"Mom!" I whispered, darting over to her. "What did they do to you?"

"Grrrmmppfffmmmpt!" she said, straining at the gag in her mouth.

Working quickly, I freed her from her bonds. Isabelle took a deep breath of air.

"Mom! Are you okay? Tell me *what* is going on," I said.

"There's no time," she gasped, standing up and brushing herself off. "We need to get to the studio."

"The *studio*? What do you mean?"

"The Fox has a TV studio in there—a three-camera soap-opera setup. If what Trish and Jeannette just said is true, they're about to do something terrible to Lisa and Charlie. And they're going to *broadcast* it."

"You mean they're going to kill them on television?" I asked.

Isabelle didn't say anything—she just gave me a look of warning.

I wanted to say about a million things to my mother. Instead I just threw my arms around her and buried my face in her neck. I don't know how, but somehow she still smelled good. She smelled . . . like my mom.

"Come on," she murmured. "We can do this."

I wished that I could stay like that forever. It had been way too long since I'd hugged my mother and actually meant it. It sucked that her kidnapping and a potential double murder were what had finally forced it. Reluctantly I pulled away and put on my game face. (Sorry for the sports metaphor. *Tiresome*, I know.)

I opened the door a crack, peering outside to make sure the coast was clear. It wasn't. Trish and Jeannette were continuing their patrol, striding along the perimeter of the island, weapons at the ready. They were headed in my direction, about to walk right past the door. And I had an idea. It was going to take good timing.

My heart was racing as the two ladies walked right past me.

One, two, three! I counted off in my mind.

I flung the heavy metal door open with every ounce of might that I had. It connected with the backs of their heads with a horrendous thud. My stomach turned as they went flying forward and lay completely still.

I had never purposely hurt anyone like that before, and I didn't like it. But I had to do what I had to do.

Trish and Jeannette were lying there, limp, on the rocks. We didn't have much time before they came to.

"Come on, Mom." I beckoned. She hurried to follow me. I bent over Trish and pulled at the shotgun trapped under her body.

My mother yelped.

"What on earth do you think you're doing?" she asked, in a scandalized tone.

"Um, we're going to need weapons," I said, staring at the butt of the gun. I had never seen a rea live firearm up close before.

"You, young lady, are underage! What kind of mother would I be if I let you run around with a loaded shotgun? You don't even know how to *use* a shotgun!" She paused and tilted her head in concern. "You *don't* know how to use a shotgun, do you?" she asked.

"Of course not," I said. "But I've seen it enough times on television. I'm sure I can figure it out."

"No! This is how accidents happen!" Isabelle snapped. "Now stand aside!"

Reluctantly I stepped to my left. Isabelle yanked the gun out from under Trish's body and emptied it of its bullets. Then she removed the arrow from Jeannette's crossbow and stashed both of them at the base of one of the boulders.

"There." She tossed her hair dramatically. "Let's go."

We made our way to the front of the hospital, Isabelle leading the way. The sun was finally gone now, and the sky was black. Creeping along, clinging to the side of the building, I couldn't stand it anymore. I needed answers.

"Mom," I whispered, "I think you should tell me what the story is here. It's the least you could do after I just sprang you."

"Oh, Lulu," she said, brushing me off. "I don't think this is the time or the place, do you?"

"No!" I said. "But it can't wait, either."

She sighed. "It's an extremely long story."

I shrugged. "Then give me the short version."

She stared at me in consternation. I looked at her impassively.

"Well," she said, "it goes something like this. For the last year, back in LA, I had been hearing rumors about this person named the Fox. She was some kind of guru who was trying to help older actresses with their careers. Of course it sounded a little peculiar to me—what kind of loon goes by a code name?—but as you know, I would never *dream* of judging another human being."

"Of course not," I said, scrambling up a rocky incline.

"So a few months ago, the Fox's people started contacting me directly. They knew of my work in film and onstage and wanted me to join their organization. I ignored their requests at first, but they were really quite persuasive. *Quite* persuasive. Flowers, chocolates—all sorts of little enticements. So I decided to meet with them. I wasn't making any promises, naturally; I just wanted to hear their proposal." She hopped nimbly over a small chasm, not missing a beat.

"When was this meeting?" I asked.

"You know," she said. "Before I got to Halo City."

"Go on," I told her.

"I discovered quickly, upon my first meeting with the Fox's ladies, that they were just completely kooky. Cream puffs, really. These women don't have minds of their own. They have been utterly, utterly brainwashed."

We had come to the main entrance to the hospital. Without hesitation Isabelle flung it open. It was empty. We dove behind an ancient nurse's desk and crouched there, keeping a lookout.

"So if you thought these people were so insane, why did you join them?"

"I didn't want to, Lulu; I didn't!" she protested. "I told Jeannette—whom I have known since her days as Scooter Rasmussen on that horrifying program—I told her, 'No, madam, I am my own woman!'"

"So what happened? What changed your mind?"

I held my breath, waiting for Isabelle to answer. I wanted to hear her say the words out loud.

"I had certain reasons," she said.

"Like what?" I pushed her. "What was your exact reason? I want to know exactly the exact reason."

Isabelle rolled her eyes. "Lulu!"

"Sorry, but I'm not going anywhere until you tell me," I said. "I'm just going to stay under this desk." *La la la, it's so comfortable and cozy under this little desk,* I sang to myself.

Of course I didn't mean it, but my mom didn't know me well enough to call my bluff.

"I did it because they were going to kidnap *you!*" she finally blurted. "I know you think I don't care about you, but I do. I stayed out of your life because you've always been happier with your father, but don't think it hasn't *pulverized* me to watch you grow up without me. And no matter how much you hate me, I'm not going to simply stand by and let someone threaten to hurt you!"

"Oh, Mom," I said.

Isabelle's eyes were suddenly miles away. "Having a child is like standing in the bottom of a burning fire pit. And you have this thing in your hands. This tiny little perfect thing. And you just need to find a way of tossing that thing up to someone out of the pit, even if it means you yourself are consumed by the raging, searing inferno."

She blinked. "You'll understand me better when you have a child of your own, Lulu. I'm sorry you don't care for me. But I'm trying to get you out of the fire pit."

A tear pricked the corner of my eye. It was another one of my mother's classic monologues. Yes, it was florid, overcooked, and kind of misguided. But it was pure Isabelle. And even if she hadn't quite gotten it all on the nose, I could tell that she really meant it, in her own ridiculous way.

I probably would have started to cry in earnest if I hadn't heard the footsteps.

Cautiously, I peeked over the desk and saw two more of the Fox's cronies walking to the door, headed outside.

I glanced at my mother. We had to hurry before they found Jeannette and Trish and were on to us. "Come on," I said as soon as they were gone. "We have to move."

In a moment we were up again, slinking through the narrow corridors, not quite knowing where we were headed.

"I love you," my mother told me as we flattened our backs to a wall and peeked around a corner into an empty hallway. It was all very "Spy vs. Spy." And she was good at it.

"I love you too," I said, and followed her move as she pressed on. "Let's just hope we don't die in the next five minutes. It would be nice to have a mother-daughter day."

"A mother-daughter day!" she exclaimed. I mean, as much as a person can *exclaim* when she's whispering. "That sounds wonderful! I've always wanted to try that!"

"As long as there's no bra shopping." I smirked, opening the next door we found. "As far as I'm concerned, that is a solitary—"

I looked up—and swallowed. Maybe I shouldn't have opened that door so quickly.

FIFTEEN "WELL, LOOK WHO

it is," a familiar voice said. "Barbie and Skipper. Just in time. It will be so much more festive with you two here!"

My mother and I had been so deep in conversation that we'd found Fiona without even really thinking about it. And it was a crazy sight to behold.

Just as my mother had said, she had converted an old office into her own personal television studio. An enormous, glaring lighting rig dangled from the ceiling, and the cameras were manned by three more of the Foxes' cookie-cutter bimbos. They were glancing at me and Isabelle nervously.

Fiona herself was sitting on a makeshift talk show set, sipping from a mug of coffee and puffing on a long, skinny cigarette. Behind her, through the window, the Halo City skyline was the brightest I'd ever seen it. Oh, wait—that's because it wasn't real. It was just an enormous photograph, gussied up to look like it was real, like on *Letterman*.

And like any good talk show, the Fox's program had "guests."

Guess who they were.

"Lulu!" Charlie exclaimed. "Thank goodness you're here!" He and Lisa were tied up in chairs, arranged interview style next to Fiona's desk.

"Yay!" Lisa cheered. "Get her, Lulu! Kick her butt!"

I would have loved to kick some booty, but at that moment, we were outnumbered—and without weapons. Given those factors, I wasn't sure what I was supposed to do.

Isabelle seemed to be having a similar dilemma.

The Fox was, understandably, unconcerned. She just sat there with an air of amusement and brushed a wayward chunk of her red mane aside.

"Two surprise guests have just joined me," she said, addressing the camera. "Let's have a warm welcome for Isabelle and Lulu Dark. They look alike, they talk alike, and they come from a whole clan of complete weenies! Could I get two extra chairs for them, please?"

And then I felt a sharp, excruciating pain against my skull. I screamed—or at least I tried to. Lisa and Charlie seemed to recede as if they were at the end of a long tunnel and I was speeding away from them. I'd been knocked out!

When I came to again, Mom and I were sitting next to Charlie and Lisa, bound tightly to wooden chairs with nylon rope. Fiona was primping in a small compact, apparently getting ready for the big show.

I was still getting my bearings, but naturally Lisa had wasted no time arguing with my mother. "I can't believe you let yourself get captured. Some rescue!"

"I'm sorry, Lisa." My mother sighed. "I really let you down."

"An apology doesn't do much good at this point!" Lisa whined. "We're all going to be dead soon!"

Oh, please. I really didn't want the final moments of my life to be wasted listening to my mother bicker with her ungrateful surrogate daughter. There had to be a way out of this mess, but this was definitely not it. I spoke up.

"I don't get it, Fiona," I said, figuring it was better to spend my efforts on the one person who could actually untie us and let us go. "What's the point of any of this? Going to jail is going to ruin your career. Why would you want to do that? You're a smart woman."

"Hold your horses, Lulu," the Fox said. "We can talk about everything in good time." She turned away from me and looked out to her camerawomen. "Are we ready to start?" she asked.

"In five! Four! Three!" one of the women shouted. She held up two fingers, then one, then pointed to Fiona. There was a burst of canned, disembodied applause through loudspeakers. Fiona preened for the camera.

"Hello, Halo City!" she said. "My name is Fiona Greer. You used to know me as the deliciously evil Patricia Berens on *Filthy Rich*, the number-one prime-time drama on television for five incredible years running. Now you may call me the Fox."

More fake applause.

"I have quite a show for you this evening," Fiona continued, gesturing at us, her prisoners. Next to me Charlie was rocking back in his chair, trying futilely to escape his bonds.

"My first guest today is Lisa Lincoln," Fiona announced. "She is a talentless and somewhat chubby young strumpet who has somehow stumbled onto fame and fortune as the ingenue of the moment."

"Chubby?" Lisa exclaimed in indignation. The Fox didn't pay any attention.

"Next I have Isabelle Dark, a constant fixture on a very small number of movie screens for the last twenty years despite her complete lack of skills or beauty."

I looked over at my mother. Always the consummate performer, she tried to make the best of the situation, tossing her hair for her "audience" and giving a winning smile.

"Hello, Fiona," she said, as if she were on a real talk show and not tied up in some kind of demented publicity stunt.

"Also joining me today is Lulu, Isabelle's sallow-faced, busybody daughter as well as the world's dumbest girl detective, along with her paramour, Charlie Reed, a rich, useless dilettante."

I tried to be offended, but I wasn't even exactly sure what *sallow-faced* meant. Anyway, it seemed like it was the least of my worries.

I looked out to the middle camera. "We're on Farmer's Island," I said. "If someone could come rescue us, I think we'd all really appreciate it."

"Don't be an idiot," Fiona snapped. "This isn't live, Lulu. We're going to distribute the tape to television stations tomorrow, after it's all over. No one is going to rescue you."

I sighed. I'd expected as much, but it had been worth a try, right?

"Now," Fiona said, "let's have a little chat. Lisa, tell me, how does it feel to know that you only have a few minutes left to live?"

Lisa looked flabbergasted. She didn't say anything.

"How informative, Lisa. You've always had a way with words. Isabelle, maybe you can answer the question. You always did like the sound of your own voice."

I had to admit she was right about that.

"Well, Fiona," my mother said, "it's a strange feeling, I must say. Having known you for almost all of my adult life, I can tell you that—"

"Ugh!" I exclaimed, cutting my mother off. "This is insane. Mom, you don't have to actually answer her questions. And Fiona, what is going on? You're going to be caught. You're recording this on video, for the love of God. Why are you doing this?"

"I'm glad you asked, Lulu!" said Fiona.

I almost burst out laughing. Of *course* she was.

"I tried to do it the easy way," she went on. "But my demands weren't met. Well, no one ignores the Fox. I won't let them. At this point you're right. I don't care whether I get away with it or not. If they won't let me be a movie star, I'll just have to make myself notorious instead. Not just famous, but *in*famous. Long after I'm gone, they'll still be—"

Okay, I was getting bored. And Fiona was obviously completely crazy—there was no reasoning with her. But what about all these women who were helping her?

"What's in it for you guys?" I asked the camerawomen. "Do you really want to spend the rest of your lives in jail?"

"Who cares?" one asked. "I haven't been able to get a job in ten years!"

"Yeah," shouted another one. "Plus what if we *don't* go to jail? I think this could really set my career on fire. Jaycee told me that your mother's getting more offers than she's gotten in the past ten years after the Halo Awards."

I looked at her. *"Jaycee?"* I asked.

Fiona was struggling to keep everything under her own control.

"*Excuse me*, ladies," she said. "But last time I checked, camera-women didn't get speaking roles."

"Why were they talking to Jaycee Frost?" I asked my mother.

She shrugged. "I think most of us have the same agent," she said. "Jaycee represents a lot of clients my age."

"Wait a minute," I said. Something wasn't right.

Unfortunately, all hell was breaking loose. There was dissent in the ranks of the Fox's henchwomen, who had turned their attention from Fiona's show and were talking among themselves. Fiona had lost control of the situation, and she wasn't happy about it.

"Excuse me!" Fiona Greer bellowed. "I'm trying to speak here. Are your little side conversations more important than what I have to say? Let's not forget who the star is. I am *the Fox*!"

"No, you're not," camerawoman number two said. "You just work for the Fox. And now you're stealing her part!"

There was more squabbling. During the confusion the final puzzle piece clicked into place. I thought I had solved this mystery. But the case wouldn't be closed until after we got off this awful island.

"Listen to me!" I pleaded to the henchwomen. "Fiona Greer doesn't care about any of you. She's only in this for herself! Why are you letting her boss you around?"

It was the right thing to say. More arguing broke out, and Fiona became more and more discombobulated.

"Psst! Lulu!" I looked over at Charlie. He had managed to untie himself! Everyone was so distracted that I was the only one who noticed.

I scooted my chair as close to his as I could, and I felt him nimbly untying my hands. Now we were getting somewhere!

"Enough!" Fiona screamed. "It's time to finish this once and for all. I'm going to be more famous than Lizzie Borden and Aileen Wuornos put together! If I can't win an Oscar for myself, maybe someone else can win one starring as me in the adaptation of my amazing true story."

She pulled a pistol from her desk and pointed it at my mother. "It didn't have to be this way, Isabelle," she said. "You could have joined us. You have no one to blame but yourself."

And then there was a bloodcurdling scream. It wasn't from my mother, or Lisa, or Charlie, or Fiona, or from any of the women in the room.

I smiled. The cavalry had arrived.

Fiona spun around, frantic, looking for the source of the noise.

Another scream.

"Girls!" Fiona said. "Please go investigate the commotion."

None of her "girls" moved.

"For God's sake," Fiona said, storming out of the room. "Do I have to take care of everything around here?"

As soon as she was out the door, the camerawomen began to

scatter, abandoning ship. The whole game had obviously gotten too out of control for all of them.

I was up in a flash, untying my mother while Charlie took care of Lisa.

I'd just gotten my mother loose when the Fox came streaking back into the room. She seemed to have dropped her gun somewhere, and I could see why she didn't look comfortable. Daisy was being dragged behind her, clinging to a chunk of her fiery hair for dear life. Daisy's T-shirt was ripped at the neck and not in a fashionable way. Her lip was bruised, and her hair was a mess. It looked like she had just fought in a war. It occurred to me that she basically *had*.

"Sorry I took so long, Lulu," she yelled. "I got a ride on some rich guy's yacht—total hottie, by the way—so what's your plan?"

"My plan is to get the hell out of here," I said.

But Fiona wasn't having it. She threw Daisy to the ground and raced over to the wall. She grabbed a thick rope and yanked hard on it.

With a huge crash the lighting rig that had been attached to the ceiling came crashing down, barely missing Daisy's head. Sparks and flame flew everywhere.

"Run for it!" I screamed.

But it was too late. Flames began shooting across the floor, blocking the doorway. They raced along the wooden boards left and right. There was no way out!

Everyone went silent.

"What now, Lu? You've got a plan, right?" my mother asked me hopefully. She turned to Lisa. "Lulu always has a plan!"

My mother's confidence was touching, but it was also unfortunately misplaced. The place was a firetrap, and our only exit was blocked by a wall of fire—it was quickly encroaching on where we stood.

"We're going down together!" Fiona cackled. She was lying on the floor, totally spent. "Tomorrow we'll all be dead, and I'll be going down in history!"

There was no use in engaging her at this point. Even if we could have reasoned with her, there wasn't anything she could have done to save us anyway.

I looked around. "Out there," I said, pointing to a pair of French doors. "Maybe we can find a way down from the balcony."

I flung open the door and stepped outside. Charlie followed close behind. It was just a tiny little overhang, three feet wide and two feet deep. I peered over the railing. We were three stories up, and below us it was all rock. We wouldn't be able to jump without breaking our necks.

"I think—I think this is it," Charlie said quietly. He looked deep into my eyes.

My heart twisted. I took his hand. "Charlie, I—"

Charlie shook his head. "It's okay. I know."

He folded me in a hug. Squeezed tightly. Just like that day on the beach. It was the biggest, most reassuring hug ever.

And then I heard a strange sound. It was a whirring, clapping roar, and it was slowly getting louder. I searched the horizon, trying to figure out where it was coming from. And then I saw: a helicopter was quickly approaching.

"Guys," I yelled. "Look!"

Daisy, Charlie, Isabelle, and Lisa rushed to my side, cramming onto the little balcony.

"What is it?" Daisy asked.

I pointed to a helicopter flying overhead. There, *hanging* from it, dangling a rope ladder, was a familiar figure.

"It's a Svenska ex machina!" Daisy gasped.

She was right. Svenska was swinging from the ladder like a pendulum. She held a bullhorn up to her mouth.

"You are ALL *grounded!"* Svenska announced.

Man, that woman has a set of lungs on her.

"This is the first time I've ever been happy to see *her*," Daisy said, smiling.

Soon the helicopter was above us. Svenska stuck out her arm and grabbed Daisy's hand, pulling her up.

And then one by one they all scrambled up until I was the last person standing on the balcony.

Yes, me. Lulu Dark. The one who is ever so slightly afraid of heights. *I* was the last one to climb the ladder.

I looked up. It was a long way to the top. I looked down. The ground didn't look very comfy. I looked behind me. The place was burning orange and red. We probably had about three minutes, tops, until the whole hospital collapsed.

"Come on!" my mother shouted from the hatch of the helicopter.

"I—I can't!" I screamed, my legs frozen in place.

"Lulu, there's no time for this!" Isabelle shouted. "I command you to get up here! I am your mother!"

I wish I could say that I was being rebellious, but that wouldn't be the truth. The truth was that I was straight-up scared. More scared than I've ever been in my life. My heart beat so hard, I felt it was going to burst out of my chest. My breathing was shallow. I couldn't get enough air.

I stood there a moment, wondering if this was how it was going to end. Then suddenly my mother was next to me.

"I'm flabbergasted that you would defy my authority like this, Lulu." Isabelle spoke softly, calmly into my ear. "Your father and I are going to have a serious talk when we get home about his permissive parenting style. But for now you *will* climb that rope." She took my chin in her hand and turned my face so that I was looking directly into her eyes. "You will climb, and I will be right behind you. I will not let you fall."

She placed my hand on the bottom rung of the ladder, which was swaying dangerously as the helicopter hovered.

Slowly I began to climb.

And as promised, Isabelle was right behind me.

The helicopter ascended into the inky black sky. Moments later there was a deafening bang. The building exploded into a gigantic fireball.

The Farmer Sanitarium for Deranged and Insane Ladies was burning to the ground.

"Can I drop you all off at your homes?" the helicopter pilot asked.

Everyone turned to stare at me. "Not yet," I told him. "First we have to find Jaycee Frost."

EPILOGUE CHARLIE AND I

went to the park. We didn't say much as we walked along the huge duck pond, riddled with rowboaters.

We had a lot of things not to talk about.

Lisa Lincoln had thrown a goodbye party the night before to celebrate her departure from Halo City—you can probably imagine that she was pretty happy to be leaving. Every famous person in town had attended the bash, not to mention everyone else in the world, including the nice people who had helped me out on the bus.

It was the fanciest party I'd ever been to. Still, I couldn't quite enjoy myself. Things just didn't seem resolved.

Yes, Lisa and Charlie and Mom were rescued. Yes, Fiona Greer was dead. And finally Jaycee Frost, the mastermind behind the entire plot, had been apprehended.

It was true: the whole plan had been Jaycee's from the start. "The Fox" was supposed to invigorate all of her clients' careers and make Jaycee the most powerful woman in Hollywood.

What Jaycee hadn't counted on was her own clients' egotism.

Fiona had hijacked the plan—and turned it into a way to settle her scores. Jaycee just couldn't control her.

Now Wanda Knight and the people in the DA's office were preparing for what would undoubtedly be dubbed the Most Amazing Kidnapping Trial of the Century! My reputation as a girl detective had spread far and wide, and I was actually pretty proud of myself.

But there were still so many things on my mind. For one thing, Charlie and I hadn't spoken since the asylum. I don't think we were mad at each other. I mean, I wasn't mad at him, and if he was still mad at me, he had a serious gratitude problem.

It was just . . . we didn't know where to start. So I'd spent the party awkwardly avoiding him, trying to act like I was having the *Most! Fun! Ever!*

It was all pretty dumb. If it hadn't been for Svenska, I wouldn't have had any fun at all. Yes, that's right—*Svenska* had been the life of the party. I don't know what had come over her, but Daisy's mom had been a firecracker all night, running around in an extremely revealing hot pink gown and causing a ruckus.

The highlight of the evening, hands down, had been her amazing karaoke duet to "Beast of Burden" with none other than La Lincoln herself. I'm telling you, you have not lived until you've seen a fifty-year-old Dutch woman swaying along with a girl a third her age, belting out a Rolling Stones classic to a crowd of scandalized glamour-pusses.

Daisy, naturally, was mortified, but the lesson that I personally took away from it was that there was more to Svenska than meets the eye. A lot more.

Anyway, that was last night. Now Charlie and I were strolling around Halo Park toward the boathouse, hoping that there was some nonverbal way of figuring out what was going on between the two of us.

It was hot, humid, and overcast, but whatever. At least it was still summer.

Charlie was wearing a slim pair of plaid seersucker shorts and a rumpled white button-down. He looked like he hadn't washed his hair in a week. He had an inscrutable look on his face.

Oh yeah, it was hot.

And what did I want, anyway? A certain part of me loved him—that was for sure. But which part was it? The dating part? Maybe. It was hard to say. I just knew that I had missed him.

"So," I said finally. "How are things with you and Lisa Lincoln?"

"Lisa Lincoln is kind of annoying," he said. "I think being kidnapped with someone can have a negative effect on the friendship. I mean, I feel like I've spent enough time with her in the last month to last me the rest of this lifetime and maybe another one after that. It's sort of a relief she went back to LA."

"Oh," I said.

"Lisa and I were just friends anyway," he told me. "I was just trying to make you jealous, you know."

"I know," I said. I *had* known, but it was nice to hear it.

I was headed to the boathouse to meet my mother for lunch. Charlie had agreed to walk me over. Just for the walk, I guess. But we were almost there, and we hadn't really gotten to discuss anything.

"Look at the ducks," I said, stumbling down off the gravel path to the muddy bank of the pond. I guess maybe I was stalling for time.

"Yep," he said. "They're very, you know, *duck-ish*. Feathers, beaks, quack quack. All of that."

"Yes," I said. "They really are."

We were silent again.

I looked off into the distance toward the boathouse. My mother was probably waiting for me on the deck.

"Well," I said.

"Well," Charlie echoed.

"Here we are," I said.

"Here we are," Charlie agreed.

"Do you want to kiss me?" I asked.

And Charlie put his hands on my hips, and pulled me to him, and kissed me . . . *on the cheek*.

Well, that answered that.

"Lulu," he said. "You know I like you. I'll always like you. And I always want to be friends. One of the reasons I like you is because you're so complicated. It makes things interesting. But when it comes to . . ." He paused, searching for the word. "When it comes to *this*, it's just too much. I'm not trying to be a game for you. Or Lisa. Or anyone. Do you see what I mean?"

"I guess," I said, even though I only half understood. I checked my watch. "I'm late."

"Well, 'bye, I guess," Charlie said. "I'll see you later?"

"Sure," I said. "Later."

"Tell your mother I said hi," he told me. "And thanks for rescuing me and all."

"Oh, Charlie," I said. I went in for another hug. But he just took a step back.

"I should go," he said.

"Okay," I said. I blinked a few times and trotted up the steps of the boathouse to meet my mother.

My mother and I sat in the heat, under an umbrella at the boathouse, nibbling halfheartedly at our sandwiches.

We talked about things like the weather, Lisa's party, reality television, and mercury in fish. In other words, a bunch of boring, pointless crap that neither of us really cared about.

But it was okay. Being a sparkling wit and a brilliant conversationalist isn't a requirement for being a good mother. The point is that Mom was trying. Maybe she had always been trying, in her way.

"So let's talk about Charlie," said Isabelle. "A little *girl talk*. I love girl talk! Don't you?"

I took a gulp of my water.

Summer was almost over. I mean, it wasn't—we were a week away from the Fourth of July. But isn't that how it always goes with summer? It's always almost over unless it's just beginning.

"Sure," I said.

I've always considered myself a truthful person. But what's a little lie every now and then?

ACKNOWLEDGMENTS

The usual thank-yous:

Thank you to Kristen Pettit for her tremendous help with the manuscript—and for putting up with me (most of the time).

Thank you to Margaret Wright for getting this ball rolling.

Thank you to Rebecca Sherman for holding my hand.

Thank you to Kristin Hagar and Erin McMonagle for being family.

Thank you to Eric Price for the good advice.

Thank you to Katie Van Wert for inspiration.

Thank you to NRDC for the coffee and the health insurance.

Thank you to Laird Adamson for everything else.